PENGUIN CLASSICS
Maigret in Court

'Extraordinary masterpieces of ⸺ ⸺
— John Banville

'A brilliant writer'   — India Knight

'Intense atmosphere and resonant detail . . . make Simenon's
fiction remarkably like life'   — Julian Barnes

'A truly wonderful writer . . . marvellously readable – lucid,
simple, absolutely in tune with the world he creates'
— Muriel Spark

'Few writers have ever conveyed with such a sure touch, the
bleakness of human life'   — A. N. Wilson

'Compelling, remorseless, brilliant'   — John Gray

'A writer of genius, one whose simplicity of language creates
indelible images that the florid stylists of our own day can
only dream of'   — *Daily Mail*

'The mysteries of the human personality are revealed in all
their disconcerting complexity'   — Anita Brookner

'One of the greatest writers of our time'   – *The Sunday Times*

'I love reading Simenon. He makes me think of Chekhov'
— William Faulkner

'One of the great psychological novelists of this century'
— *Independent*

'The greatest of all, the most genuine novelist we have had
in literature'   — André Gide

'Simenon ought to be spoken of in the same breath as
Camus, Beckett and Kafka'   — *Independent on Sunday*

GEORGES SIMENON

Maigret in Court

Translated by ROS SCHWARTZ

PENGUIN BOOKS

PENGUIN CLASSICS

UK | USA | Canada | Ireland | Australia
India | New Zealand | South Africa

Penguin Books is part of the Penguin Random House group of companies
whose addresses can be found at global.penguinrandomhouse.com.

Penguin
Random House
UK

First published in French as *Maigret aux assises* by Presses de la Cité 1960
This translation first published 2018
004

Set in 12.5/15 pt Dante MT Std
Typeset by Jouve (UK), Milton Keynes

Printed and bound in Great Britain by Clays Ltd, Elcograf S.p.A.

ISBN: 978-0-141-98591-6

www.greenpenguin.co.uk

Maigret in Court

1.

How many times had he been here, two hundred? Three hundred? Even more? He had no wish to count or to remember every single case, even the most notorious, the ones that had gone down in the annals of legal history, because this was the most distasteful side of his profession.

But didn't most of his investigations end up in court, like today? He would have preferred not to know, or at least to remain at a remove from these last rites to which he had never become fully accustomed.

In his office at Quai des Orfèvres, the battles that generally ended in the small hours were a struggle between one man and another, on an equal footing so to speak.

A few corridors away, a few flights of stairs, and it was a different scenario, a different world, where words no longer had the same meaning – an abstract, monastic world that was both austere and absurd.

Along with the other witnesses, he had just left the dark-wood panelled courtroom where the glow from the electric globe lights dissolved into the greyness of a rainy afternoon. The elderly usher, who had been the same age for as long as Maigret had known him, showed them into a smaller room, like a schoolmaster leading his pupils, and gestured towards the benches screwed to the walls.

Most of the witnesses meekly sat down, obeying the instructions of the presiding judge, not saying a word, reluctant even to look at their companions.

They stared straight ahead, tense, withdrawn, keeping their secrets for the solemn moment later on when, alone in an intimidating courtroom, they would be cross-examined.

It was a little like the sacristy of a church. As a boy Maigret used to serve mass every morning at the village church and now he experienced the same anxiety as when he was waiting to follow the priest to the altar lit by flickering candle flames. He could hear the footsteps of the invisible worshippers taking their seats, the comings and goings of the sacristan.

In the same way, he was able to follow the ritual ceremony taking place on the other side of the door. He recognized the voice of Judge Bernerie, the most meticulous and pernickety of the magistrates, but perhaps also the most scrupulous and the most determined to root out the truth. Thin and sickly looking, with a dry cough and feverish eyes, he resembled a stained-glass-window image of a saint.

Then came the voice of Aillevard, who sat on the prosecution bench.

Lastly, footsteps could be heard, those of the court usher who, opening the door to the courtroom a fraction, called:

'Detective Chief Inspector Segré.'

Segré, who had not sat down, glanced over at Maigret and entered the courtroom in his overcoat, holding his grey hat. The others gazed at him for a moment, thinking that soon it would be their turn and wondering anxiously how they would conduct themselves.

A patch of colourless sky was visible through the windows, which were so high up they had to be opened and closed with a cord, and the electric light sculpted the faces with their blank stares.

The room was warm, but it would have been inappropriate for Maigret to remove his overcoat. There were certain court rituals that were sacrosanct, and it made no difference that Maigret was a neighbour and had made his way to the court along the dusky corridors of the Palais de Justice: he kept his coat on and held his hat in his hands like all the others.

It was October. Maigret had only returned from his holiday two days earlier, to a Paris deluged by rain that felt as if it would never stop. He had gone home to Boulevard Richard-Lenoir, and then to his office, with an indefinable feeling, a sort of mixture of pleasure and sorrow.

Earlier, when the judge had asked him his age, he had replied:

'Fifty-three.'

Which meant that he would be forced to retire in two years' time, in accordance with the regulations.

He had often thought about stopping, and usually with joyful anticipation. But this time, coming back from holiday, retirement was no longer a vague or distant thought; it was a logical, inevitable and imminent reality.

During their three weeks in the Loire region, the future

had become concrete when the Maigrets had finally bought the house where they would spend their old age.

They had done so almost half-heartedly. As in previous years, they had stayed at a hotel in Meung-sur-Loire where they felt at home, and where the owners, the Fayets, treated them as part of the family.

Posters on the walls of the little town advertised the auction of a house on the edge of the countryside. He and Madame Maigret went to visit it. The property was very ancient and had a grey-walled garden. It reminded them of a presbytery.

They had been charmed by the blue-tiled corridors, the kitchen with its heavy beams, which was three steps below ground level and still had a pump in a corner; the sitting room smelled like the parlour of a convent and the leaded windows broke up the sun's rays, creating mysterious light patterns.

At the auction, the Maigrets, standing at the back of the room, had looked at each other questioningly and had both been surprised when Maigret raised his hand, while the local farmers turned around . . . 'Going . . . Going . . . Gone!'

For the first time in their lives, they were property owners and, the very next day, they brought in a plumber and a carpenter.

They had even spent the remaining days of their holiday visiting local antiques shops. They bought, among other things, a firewood box emblazoned with the coat of arms of Francis I. They put it in the hallway by the door of the sitting room, which had a stone hearth.

Maigret hadn't mentioned the house to Janvier or Lucas, or to anyone, almost as if he were ashamed to be planning for the future, as if it were a betrayal of Quai des Orfèvres.

The previous day, he'd had the impression that his office wasn't exactly the same and, this morning, in the witnesses' room, listening to the sounds from the courtroom, he was beginning to feel like an outsider.

In two years' time, he'd be fishing, and on winter afternoons he'd probably go and play cards with the locals in a corner of the café where he too was becoming a regular.

Judge Bernerie asked very precise questions to which the inspector from the 9th arrondissement gave equally precise replies.

The witnesses on the benches around Maigret had all passed through his office, some of them spending several hours there. Was it because these men and women were intimidated by their imposing surroundings that they appeared not to recognize him?

True, he would not be the one cross-examining them. They were no longer facing a man like themselves but an impersonal machine, and it wasn't even certain that they would understand the questions put to them.

The door opened a crack. It was his turn. Like his colleague from the 9th arrondissement, he held his hat in his hand as he made his way towards the semi-circular witness stand, looking straight ahead.

'Your surname, forenames, age and profession . . .'

'Maigret, Jules, fifty-three years old, divisional chief inspector of the Paris Police Judiciaire.'

'You are not related to the defendant or employed by him . . . Raise your right hand . . . Swear to tell the truth, the whole truth and nothing but the truth.'

'I swear.'

To his right, he saw the profiles of the jury, their faces pale in the gloom and, to his left, behind the lawyers in their black gowns, the defendant, flanked by two uniformed guards, his chin resting on his folded hands, staring at him intently.

The two of them had spent long hours face to face in the stiflingly hot office at Quai des Orfèvres, and they had broken off the interrogation to have a sandwich and a beer, chatting like old friends.

'Now look, Meurant . . .'

Perhaps Maigret had occasionally called him Gaston?

Here, there was an unsurmountable barrier between them, and Gaston Meurant's expression was as neutral as Maigret's.

Judge Bernerie and Maigret also knew one another, not only from having chatted in the corridors but because this was the thirtieth cross-examination to which the judge had subjected Maigret.

There was no hint of any of that. Each played his part as if they were strangers, the officiants of a ceremony as ancient and ritualistic as mass.

'Can you confirm that it was you, inspector, who wrote the investigation report on the case before the court?'

'Yes, your honour.'

'Face the gentlemen of the jury and tell them what you know.'

'On 28 February last, at around one o'clock, I was in my office at Quai des Orfèvres when I received a telephone call from the chief of the 9th arrondissement. He told me a murder had just been discovered in Rue Manuel, around the corner from Rue des Martyrs, and that he was on his way to the scene. A few moments later, I had a phone call from the public prosecutor's office instructing me to go there as well and to send experts from Criminal Records and forensics.'

Maigret heard coughs and, behind him, feet tapping the floor. It was the first case of the term and every seat was filled. There were probably spectators standing at the back, near the big door guarded by uniformed men.

Judge Bernerie belonged to that minority of magistrates who applied the Criminal Procedure Code to the letter. He was not content for the court merely to listen to a summary of the investigation but would comb through it in fine detail.

'Did you find the public prosecutor at the scene?'

'I arrived a few minutes before the deputy public prosecutor. Detective Chief Inspector Segré was there, accompanied by his secretary and two neighbourhood inspectors. No one had touched anything.'

'Tell us what your saw.'

'Rue Manuel is a quiet, middle-class street, with very little traffic, which runs into the bottom of Rue des Martyrs. Number 27a is an apartment building about halfway down. The concierge's lodge is not on the ground floor but on the mezzanine. The officer waiting for me showed me up to the second floor where I saw two doors that opened on to the landing. The one on the right was ajar and on a little copper plate was the name "Madame Faverges".'

Maigret knew that, for Judge Bernerie, every little detail mattered and that he should omit nothing, otherwise he would be reprimanded.

'I noticed nothing untoward in the hallway, which was lit by a frosted-glass electric lamp.'

'One moment. Did the door show any signs of a break-in?'

'No. It was examined later by the experts and the lock was taken apart. It was established that none of the tools generally used for breaking and entering had been used.'

'Thank you. Continue.'

'The apartment comprises four rooms, as well as the hallway. Opposite it is a sitting room with glass doors hung with cream-coloured curtains. It was in that room, which has another glass door opening into the dining room, that I saw the two bodies.'

'Where were they exactly?'

'That of the woman, whom I later learned was called Léontine Faverges, was lying on the rug, her head turned towards the window. Her throat had been slit with an instrument which was no longer in the room, and on the rug was a pool of blood more than fifty centimetres in diameter. As for the body of the child . . .'

'That was young Cécile Perrin, aged four, who normally lived with Léontine Faverges, was it not?'

'Yes, your honour. Her body was curled up on a Louis XV settee, her face buried under the silk cushions. As the neighbourhood doctor stated and Doctor Paul confirmed a little later, after being partially strangled, the child was suffocated with the cushions . . .'

A murmur rippled through the room, but the judge simply looked up and glared at the rows of spectators, and silence reigned once more.

'After the arrival of the prosecutor, did you and your colleagues stay in the apartment until the evening?'

'Yes, your honour.'

'Tell us what observations you made.'

Maigret only hesitated for a few seconds.

'I was immediately struck by the furniture and the décor. Léontine Faverges' ID documents state that she was unemployed. She lived on a small private income, taking care of Cécile Perrin, whose mother, a cabaret hostess, was unable to look after her.'

On entering the courtroom, he had spotted the child's mother, Juliette Perrin, sitting in the front row of the public gallery, because she was the person who had brought the civil proceedings. She had dyed auburn hair and wore a fur coat.

'Tell us exactly what struck you about the apartment.'

'An unusual attention to detail, a particular style that reminded me of certain apartments from the days before the prostitution laws. The sitting room, for example, was too muted, too soft, with its profusion of rugs and cushions and prints of romantic scenes on the walls. The lampshades were in pastel colours, as they were in the two bedrooms where there were more mirrors than is customary. I subsequently found out that in the past

Léontine Faverges had used her apartment as a brothel. After the enactment of the new laws, she continued for a while. The Vice Squad had to get involved and it was only after being fined several times that she accepted she would have to cease her activities.'

'Have you been able to establish what her financial situation was?'

'According to the concierge, neighbours and everyone who knew her, she had savings, because she'd never been a spendthrift. Her maiden name was Meurant – she was the sister of the defendant's mother. She arrived in Paris at the age of eighteen and worked as a sales assistant in a department store for a spell. At twenty, she married a man called Faverges, a sales representative, who died three years later in an automobile accident. The couple lived in Asnières at the time. For a few years, the young woman was seen haunting the brasseries in Rue Royale and she has a record with the Vice Squad.'

'Did you investigate whether among the people she used to mix with in those days there was anyone who might have remembered her recently and attacked her?'

'The people who knew her considered her something of a loner, which is quite unusual. She saved her money, which is how she was eventually able to afford to move to Rue Manuel.'

'She was sixty-two at the time of her death?'

'Yes. She had grown fat, but as far as I can judge, she was still youthful-looking and conscious of her appearance. The witnesses we questioned said that she was very fond of the little girl who was living with her, not so much for the small income it brought her but because she kept her company.'

'Did she have a bank or post-office account?'

'No. She was suspicious of financial establishments, lawyers and investments in general, and she kept everything she had in her home.'

'Was any money found?'

'Very little – some small change and low-denomination notes in a handbag, and more coins in a kitchen drawer.'

'Did she have a hiding place, and did you find it?'

'Apparently she did. When Léontine Faverges was ill, which she was on two or three occasions in recent years, the concierge would go up and do her cleaning and take care of the child. On a chest in the sitting room there was a Chinese vase filled with artificial flowers. One day, the concierge took them out to dust them and in the bottom of the vase she found a cotton pouch that appeared to contain gold coins. Judging from the size and weight, the concierge claims that there were more than a thousand coins. We conducted an experiment in my office, with a cotton pouch and a thousand coins. The result seemed conclusive. I had the employees of the various local banks questioned. At the Crédit Lyonnais they recalled a woman matching Léontine Faverges' description who allegedly bought bearer shares on several occasions. One of the clerks, called Durat, formally identified her from her photograph.'

'So it's likely that those shares were kept in the apartment along with the gold coins. But you didn't find anything?'

'No, your honour. Naturally we looked for fingerprints on the Chinese vase, on the drawers and just about everywhere in the apartment.'

'And you didn't find any?'

'Only the prints of the two occupants and, in the kitchen, those of a delivery boy whose movements were verified. His last delivery was on the morning of the 27th. But according to Doctor Paul, who performed both autopsies, the murder took place between five and eight in the evening on 27 February.'

'Did you question all the residents of the building?'

'Yes, your honour. They confirmed what the concierge had already told me, in other words that Léontine Faverges received no male visitors apart from her two nephews.'

'Could you tell us about the defendant, Gaston Meurant, and his brother Alfred?'

'The concierge stated that Gaston Meurant came to see his aunt fairly regularly, once or twice a month, and that his last visit had been about three weeks earlier. As for the brother, Alfred Meurant, he only put in very rare appearances at Rue Manuel because his aunt disapproved of him. On questioning the neighbour opposite, Madame Solange Lorris, a dressmaker, I learned that one of her customers had come to see her for a fitting on 27 February, at five thirty. This person is called Madame Ernie and lives in Rue Saint-Georges. She states that as she was walking up the stairs a man came out of the dead woman's apartment and, on seeing her, appeared to change his mind. Instead of going down the stairs, he headed for the third floor.

She wasn't able to see his face because the staircase is poorly lit. She described the man as wearing a navy-blue suit and a brown belted raincoat.'

'Tell us how you came into contact with the defendant.'

'While my men and I were searching the apartment on the afternoon of 28 February and starting to question the residents, the evening papers reported the murder and gave a certain number of details.'

'Just a moment. How was the crime discovered?'

'At around midday that day, I mean 28 February, the concierge was surprised not to have seen either Léontine Faverges or the little girl, who attended a local nursery school. She went up and rang the bell. Having received no reply, she returned a little later and there was still no answer. Finally, she telephoned the police. To go back to Gaston Meurant: the concierge knew only that he was a picture-framer and that he lived near Père-Lachaise. I didn't need to track him down because the next morning . . .'

'That would be 1 March . . .'

'Yes. The next morning, as I was saying, he presented himself of his own accord at the police station of the 9th arrondissement saying he was the victim's nephew, and they sent him over to me . . .'

Judge Bernerie was not one of those judges who took notes or dealt with their correspondence during a hearing, nor did he snooze. His gaze flitted constantly from the witness to the defendant, with the occasional glance in the direction of the jury.

'Tell us as exactly as possible about your first interview with Gaston Meurant.'

'He was dressed in a grey suit and a shabby beige rain-coat. He seemed intimidated to find himself in my office and I had the impression that it was his wife who had urged him to come forward.'

'Was she with him?'

'She stayed in the waiting room. One of my inspectors came and informed me and I invited her in. Meurant told me that he'd read the papers, that Léontine Faverges was his aunt and, since he and his brother were the victim's only relatives as far as he knew, he believed he had a duty to make himself known to the police. I asked him about his relationship with the old lady and he told me that they had been on excellent terms. In response to further questioning he added that his last visit to Rue Manuel had been on 23 January. He was not able to give me the address of his brother, from whom he was estranged.'

'So, on 1 March, the defendant categorically denied having been at Rue Manuel on 27 February, the day of the murder.'

'Yes, your honour. When questioned about his movements, he told me he had worked in his studio in Rue de la Roquette until six thirty. I subsequently visited this studio, as well as the shop, which has a narrow window and is cluttered with frames and engravings. There's a suction hook behind the glass door for a sign saying: "If I am not here, please come to the studio across the court-yard." An unlit passageway leads to the studio where Meurant made his frames.'

'Is there a concierge?'

'No. The place only has two floors, reached by a staircase from the courtyard. It is a very old building, sandwiched between two lodging houses.'

One of the judge's assistants, whom Maigret did not know because he had recently arrived from the provinces, looked straight ahead at the public in front of him, appearing not to hear anything. The other, by contrast, rosy-cheeked and white-haired, nodded his approval of Maigret's every word, occasionally giving a contented smile for some strange reason. The jury meanwhile sat there as motionless as if they had been painted plaster figures in a nativity scene.

The counsel for the defence, Pierre Duché, was young and this was his first big case. On edge, as if always about to pounce, he pored over his paperwork, covering it with annotations.

Only Gaston Meurant appeared to be detached from what was going on around him or, to be more precise, attended this performance as if it had nothing to do with him.

He was thirty-eight, on the tall side, with broad shoulders and curly ginger hair, the complexion of a redhead and blue eyes.

All the witnesses described him as a mild, calm man, not very sociable, who divided his time between his studio in Rue de la Roquette and his home on Boulevard de Charonne, which overlooked Père-Lachaise cemetery.

He was rather typical of the solitary craftsman, and if there was anything surprising about him, it was the wife he had chosen.

Ginette Meurant was petite and very curvaceous, with a come-hither look in her eye, a suggestive pout and seductive manner.

Ten years her husband's junior, she appeared even younger than her age, and had a habit of fluttering her eyelashes as if bewildered.

'What did the defendant tell you about his movements between five and eight in the evening on 27 February?'

'He told me he left his studio at around six thirty, switched off the lights in the shop and walked home as usual. His wife wasn't there. She had gone to the cinema, to the five o'clock showing, which she often does. We have the testimony of the box-office cashier. It was a cinema in Faubourg Saint-Antoine, where she's a regular. When she got home, just before eight, her husband had cooked dinner and set the table.'

'Was that usual?'

'Apparently.'

'Did the concierge at Boulevard de Charonne see her arrive?'

'She doesn't remember. There are some twenty apartments in the building and there are a lot of comings and goings in the late afternoon.'

'Did you talk to the defendant about the vase, the gold coins and the bearer shares?'

'Not on that occasion but the next day, 2 March, when I summoned him to my office. I had only just been told about the money by the concierge from Rue Manuel.'

'Did the defendant seem to know about it?'

'He hesitated at first, and then he finally admitted that he did.'

'Had his aunt told him her secret?'

'Indirectly. At this point I must digress briefly. Around five years ago, under pressure from his wife apparently, Gaston Meurant abandoned his profession to buy a café-restaurant business in Rue du Chemin-Vert.'

'Why do you say "under pressure from his wife"?'

'Because when Meurant first got to know her, eight years ago, she was a waitress in a restaurant in Faubourg Saint-Antoine. Meurant was a customer there and that's how they met. He married her and, she claims, insisted she stop working. Meurant acknowledges that's true. But Ginette Meurant's ambition was still to be the owner of a café-restaurant one day and when the opportunity arose, she urged her husband . . .'

'Was it a bad deal?'

'Yes. Within months, Meurant had to ask his aunt to lend him some money.'

'Did she?'

'Several times. According to her nephew, in the Chinese vase there were not just gold coins but an old wallet containing banknotes. She took the money she lent him from the wallet. She jokingly called the vase her Chinese safe.'

'Did you track down the defendant's brother, Alfred Meurant?'

'Not at the time. I merely knew from our records that he led an irregular life and that he had been convicted twice for procuring.'

'Did any witnesses testify that they had seen the defendant in his studio after five o'clock on the afternoon of the murder?'

'Not at the time.'

'Was he wearing, according to him, a blue suit and a brown raincoat?'

'No. His everyday suit, which is grey, and a light-beige gabardine that he usually wore to go to work.'

'If I understand correctly, there was no specific evidence enabling you to charge him?'

'That is correct.'

'Can you tell us what the focus of your investigation was during the days following the murder?'

'First of all, it was on the past of the victim, Léontine Faverges, and that of the men she had known. We also inquired about friends the girl's mother, Juliette Perrin, who knew about the contents of the Chinese vase and could have told others about it.'

'Did this lead anywhere?'

'No. We also questioned all the neighbours in the street, anyone who might have seen the murderer walk past.'

'To no avail?'

'To no avail.'

'So that, by the morning of 6 March, the investigation had stalled.'

'That is correct.'

'What happened on the morning of 6 March?'

'I was in my office at around ten o'clock when I received a telephone message.'

'Who was the caller?'

'I don't know. The person wouldn't give their name and I signalled to Inspector Janvier, sitting next to me, to try and trace the call.'

'Did he succeed in doing so?'

'No. The conversation was too short. I simply recognized the tell-tale click of a public telephone.'

'Was it a man or a woman who called you?'

'A man. I could swear he was talking through a handkerchief to disguise his voice.'

'What did he say to you?'

'Verbatim: "If you want to know who the Rue Manuel murderer is, ask Meurant to show you his blue suit. You'll see bloodstains on it."'

'What did you do?'

'I went to see the examining magistrate, who issued me with a search warrant. Inspector Janvier accompanied me and we arrived at Boulevard de Charonne at ten past eleven. We went up to the third floor and I rang the bell of the Meurants' apartment. Madame Meurant opened the door. She was in her dressing gown and slippers. She told us her husband was in his studio and I asked her if he owned a blue suit.

'"Of course," she replied. "It's his Sunday best."

'I asked to see it. The apartment is comfortable, stylish and cheerful, but at that hour it was still untidy.

'"Why do you want to see that suit?"

'"A routine formality . . ."

'I followed her into the bedroom and she took the navy-blue suit out of the wardrobe. Then I showed her the search warrant. We put the suit in a special bag that I'd brought and Inspector Janvier filled out the usual forms.

'Half an hour later, the suit was in the hands of the

forensics team. During the afternoon, I was informed that it did indeed have traces of blood on the right sleeve and on the cuff, but that I would have to wait until the following day to find out whether it was human blood. From midday, however, I had Gaston Meurant and his wife put under discreet surveillance.

'The next morning, 7 March, two of my men, Inspectors Janvier and Lapointe, arrived at the studio in Rue de la Roquette armed with an arrest warrant, and proceeded to apprehend Gaston Meurant.

'He seemed surprised. He put up no resistance and said:

'"This must be a misunderstanding."

'I was waiting for him in my office. His wife, in an adjacent room, was more anxious than he was.'

'Can you, without referring to your notes, repeat the substance of your interview of the defendant that day?'

'I believe I can, your honour. I was sitting at my desk and I left him standing. Inspector Janvier stood next to him while Inspector Lapointe sat down in order to take notes.

'I was busy signing letters and that took quite some time. I finally looked up and said in a reprimanding tone:

'"This is not good, Meurant. Why did you lie to me?"

'His ears turned red and his lips twitched.

'"Until now," I went on, "I didn't consider you a possible culprit, not even a suspect. But what do you expect me to think now that I know you went to Rue Manuel on 27 February? Why did you go there? Why did you keep quiet about it?"'

The judge leaned forward so as not to miss a word of what was to come.

'What did he reply?'

'He stammered and hung his head: "I am innocent. They were already dead."'

2.

The judge must have discreetly beckoned the clerk, who walked silently around the bench and leaned over to him, while Duché, the young counsel for the defence, pale and tense, tried to fathom what was happening.

The judge said a few brief words and everyone in the room followed his gaze as it rested on the high windows from which long cords dangled.

The radiators were scalding hot. With so many people pressed together, the air was stale and there was a growing smell of body odour, damp clothes and bad breath.

Like a doddery sacristan, the clerk went over to one of the cords and tried to open a window. It was jammed. He made three attempts and everything remained in suspense, all eyes upon him, then there was a nervous laugh when he decided to try the next window.

Because of this episode, on seeing rivulets of rain on the windowpanes and clouds in the sky, and suddenly hearing cars and buses braking more clearly, people became conscious of the outside world again. At that precise moment, they could even hear the siren of an ambulance or police car punctuating the silence.

Maigret waited, anxious, focused. He had taken advantage of the pause to glance over at Meurant, who met his gaze, and he thought he could read a reprimand in the defendant's blue eyes.

This was not the first time that in the same witness box Maigret had felt a certain despondency. In his office at Quai des Orfèvres, he was still grappling with reality and, even when writing his report, he was able to believe that his words reflected the truth.

Then months went by, sometimes a year, if not two, and one fine day he found himself penned in the witness room with people he had questioned in the past and who were no more than a memory for him. Were these really the same human beings – concierges, passers-by and tradesmen – who were sitting there on the vestry benches, staring vacantly?

After months in prison, was that the same man in the dock?

They suddenly found themselves in an impersonal world, where everyday words no longer seemed to mean anything, where the most mundane details were translated into unintelligible formulae. The judges' black gowns, the ermine, the prosecutor's red robe further added to the impression of a ceremony set in stone where the individual counted for nothing.

Judge Bernerie, however, led the proceedings with the utmost patience and humanity. He did not put pressure on the witnesses to finish, nor did he interrupt them when they got bogged down in unnecessary detail.

With other, stricter magistrates, Maigret would sometimes clench his fists in anger and helplessness.

Even today, he knew that he was only giving a lifeless,

simplified picture. Everything he had just said was true, but he hadn't conveyed the full weight of things, their density, their texture, their smell.

For example, he felt it was essential for those who were going to judge Gaston Meurant to experience the atmosphere of the apartment on Boulevard de Charonne as he had found it.

His two-sentence description was useless. He had been struck, right away, by the couple's home in that large apartment building overlooking the cemetery, full of families and children.

Who had chosen the décor and the furnishings? In the bedroom there wasn't a proper bed but one of those corner divans surrounded by a shelving unit known as a cosy-corner. It was covered in orange satin.

Maigret tried to imagine the picture-framer, the craftsman busy all day in his studio at the far end of a courtyard, coming home from work to this interior out of a glossy magazine: lights almost as soft as the ones in Rue Manuel, furniture that was too pale, too shiny, and pastel colours . . .

And yet, it was Meurant's books that were on the shelves, nothing but second-hand books from one of the stalls by the Seine: Tolstoy's *War and Peace*; eighteen bound volumes of *History of the Consulate and the Empire* in an ancient edition that smelled of must; *Madame Bovary*; a work on wild animals and, next to it, a *History of Religions*.

You could tell he was a man trying to educate himself. In the same room were piles of romance digests, colourful magazines, film reviews and trashy novels that probably constituted Ginette Meurant's diet, like the records by the gramophone that all bore the titles of sentimental songs.

How did the two of them spend their evenings and their Sundays? What did they say to one another? How did they behave?

Maigret was also conscious of not having given a precise idea either of Léontine Faverges or of her apartment where gentlemen who had families, a reputation, used to make discreet visits and were concealed behind thick curtains to avoid their meeting one another.

'*I am innocent. They were already dead . . .*'

In the courtroom, which was as full as a cinema, that sounded like a desperate lie because for the public, who only knew what they had read about the case in the newspapers, and for the jury too, Gaston Meurant was indisputably a killer who had had no qualms about attacking a little girl, trying firstly to strangle her and then, panicked because she didn't die fast enough, suffocating her under a pile of silk cushions.

It was barely eleven o'clock, but did the people in the courtroom now have any sense of time, or even of their own personal lives? Among the jury was a bird-seller from Quai de la Mégisserie and a plumbing contractor who worked alongside his two employees.

Was there also among them someone who had married a woman like Ginette Meurant and who at night read the same sort of books as the defendant?

'Go on, detective chief inspector.'

'I asked him about his exact movements on the

afternoon of 27 February. At two o'clock, he opened his shop as usual and hung the sign on the back of the door saying to go through to the studio. He went over to his studio and worked on several frames. At four, he lit the lamps and went back into the shop to turn on the lights in the window. He was still in his studio when, just after six, he heard footsteps in the courtyard. There was a knock on the window.

'It was an elderly gentleman, whom he claims never to have seen before. He wanted a flat, 40 × 55 centimetre Romantic-style frame for an Italian watercolour he had just bought. Meurant said he showed him mouldings of different widths. After inquiring about the price, the elderly gentleman left, according to him.'

'Has this witness been found?'

'Yes, your honour. Just three weeks. He is a certain Germain Lombras, piano teacher, who lives in Rue Picpus.'

'Did you question him yourself?'

'Yes, your honour. He confirms that he did indeed go to Meurant's studio one evening, just after six. He happened to be passing the shop, having bought a Neapolitan land-scape from a second-hand goods dealer the previous day.'

'Did he tell you what the defendant was wearing?'

'He said that Meurant was wearing grey trousers under beige overalls, and had removed his tie.'

Aillevard on the prosecution bench was following Mai-gret's testimony in the file open in front of him. He made a move to ask for permission to speak, and Maigret hastily added:

'The witness was unable to say whether this scene took place on the Tuesday or the Wednesday, i.e. on 26 or 27 February.'

Now it was the turn of the defence counsel to become anxious. The young lawyer, generally predicted to have a brilliant future ahead of him, was risking his entire career with this case. He must, at all costs, give the impression of being sure of himself and of the cause he was defending, and he made every effort to control the shaking hands which betrayed him.

Maigret went on in a neutral tone:

'The defendant claims that, after this visit, he locked up the studio, then the shop, and walked to the bus stop.'

'Which means he would have left at approximately six thirty?'

'Around that time. He got off the bus at the bottom of Rue des Martyrs and walked to Rue Manuel.'

'Did he have any specific reason for visiting his aunt?'

'At first, he told me he didn't, that it was just a normal visit. He was in the habit of going to see her at least once a month. Two days later, however, when we found out about the unpaid bank draft, he retracted his statement.'

'Tell us about that bank draft.'

'On the 28th, Meurant was due to pay a rather large bank draft, which had already been blocked the previous month because he didn't have the necessary funds.'

'Was this draft presented?'

'Yes.'

'Was it paid?'

'No.'

The assistant public prosecutor seemed to sweep this argument in Meurant's favour aside, whereas Pierre Duché turned to the jury as if asking them to take note.

The fact had worried Maigret too. If after slitting his aunt's throat and suffocating little Cécile Perrin the defendant had stolen the gold coins and banknotes hidden in the Chinese vase, if he had taken the bearer shares too, why, given that he was not yet under suspicion, and might have thought that he never would be, had he not paid the draft, since he risked being declared bankrupt?

'My inspectors calculated how long it would take to get from Rue de la Roquette to Rue Manuel. At that time of day, it takes around half an hour by bus or twenty minutes by taxi. Questioning the taxi-drivers led nowhere; the same with the bus-drivers. No one remembers Meurant.

'According to his successive statements, which he signed, he arrived at Rue Manuel a few minutes before seven o'clock. He met no one on the stairs, and didn't see the concierge. He knocked on his aunt's door, but there was no reply. He was surprised to find the key in the lock.

'He went in and found himself confronted with the scene described earlier.'

'Were the lights on?'

'The big standard lamp in the sitting room with a salmon-pink shade was on. Meurant believes there were lights on in the other rooms, but that is only an impression, because he didn't go into them.'

'What explanation does he give for his behaviour? Why did he not bother to call a doctor or inform the police?'

'He was afraid he'd be accused. He saw that one of the

Louis XV desk drawers was open, and closed it. He also put the artificial flowers that were strewn on the floor back in the Chinese vase. On leaving, he realized that he may have left some fingerprints, and so he wiped the desk and then the vase with his handkerchief. He also wiped the door handle and took the key before going down the stairs.'

'What did he do with it?'

'He threw it down a drain.'

'How did he get back home?'

'By bus. The route to Boulevard de Charonne is via streets that are not too busy and apparently he was home by seven thirty-five.'

'Wasn't his wife there?'

'No. As I said, she had gone to the five o'clock screening at a local cinema. She went to the cinema a lot, almost every day. Five box-office cashiers recognized her when they were shown her photo. While he waited for her, Meurant heated up the leftovers of a leg of lamb and some green beans, then he set the table.'

'Did he do that often?'

'Very often.'

Although Meurant had his back to the public, he had the feeling that everyone was smiling, especially the women.

'How many times did you question the defendant?'

'Five times, once for eleven hours. He stood by his story, so I wrote my report and handed it to the examining magistrate. I have not had the opportunity to see him again since.'

'Did he not write to you once he was in prison?'

'Yes. The letter is in the file. He states once again that he is innocent and asks me to watch over his wife.'

Maigret avoided looking at Meurant, who had made a slight movement.

'He doesn't say what he means by that, or what he fears for her?'

'No, your honour.'

'Did you find his brother?'

'Two weeks after the murders in Rue Manuel, on 14 March to be precise.'

'In Paris?'

'In Toulon, where he spends most of his time, although he has no permanent address there. He often makes trips to the Riviera, either to Marseille, or Nice and Menton. He was interrogated initially by the Toulon Police Judiciaire, to whom we had sent a letter of request. Then, summoned to my office, he came, not without demanding that his travel expenses be paid in advance. He claimed he hadn't set foot in Paris since January and gave the names of three witnesses with whom he was playing cards in Bandol on 27 February. The witnesses were questioned. They belong to the same milieu as Alfred Meurant, in other words, organized crime.'

'What date did you deliver your report to the examining magistrate?'

'The final report, as well as the various statements signed by the defendant, were handed over on 28 March.'

Now they were getting to the delicate moment. Only three of them knew it, and some of them had an important role in the proceedings. First of all, the public prosecutor,

Justin Aillevard, whom Maigret had visited at five o'clock the previous day in his office. Then, as well as Maigret himself, Judge Bernerie, also informed later the previous evening by the assistant public prosecutor.

But there were others who were also waiting for that moment, unbeknown to the public: five inspectors, hand-picked by Maigret from among those who were less well known, some of them from the Vice Squad.

They had been at strategic points in the room since the start of the trial, mingling with the crowd, watching people's faces and noting their reactions.

'And so officially, detective chief inspector, your investigation ended on 28 March.'

'That is correct.'

'And since that date, have you nevertheless taken an interest in the doings of people associated with the defendant, either closely or remotely?'

The counsel for the defence sprang to his feet, ready to protest. He was probably going to say that it was not acceptable to bring up evidence against his client that was not in the file.

'Don't worry, maître,' the judge reassured him. 'You will see in a minute that if I am using my discretionary powers to refer to an unforeseen turn in the case, it is not with the intention of prejudicing the defendant.'

Meanwhile, the assistant public prosecutor shot the young defence lawyer a slightly ironic, half-protective look.

'I repeat my question. Did Detective Chief Inspector Maigret unofficially pursue his investigation?'

'Yes, your honour.'

'On your own initiative?'

'With the agreement of the chief superintendent of the Police Judiciaire.'

'Did you inform the public prosecutor?'

'Only yesterday, your honour.'

'Did the examining magistrate know that you were still involved in the case?'

'I talked to him about it in passing.'

'However, you were acting neither on his instructions, nor on those of the public prosecutor?'

'No, your honour.'

'It is necessary for that to be clearly established. That is why I described this further investigation as unofficial. For what reason, detective chief inspector, did you continue to deploy your inspectors in pursuit of a case once it had been referred to the court?'

The quality of the silence in the room had changed. Not the faintest cough was heard and not a single foot tapped the floor.

'I was dissatisfied with the findings,' grunted Maigret.

He couldn't explain exactly what it was that had troubled him. The word *dissatisfied* was utterly inadequate. The facts, he felt, did not tally with the characters. How could he explain that in the solemn setting of a courtroom, where he was asked to speak in precise sentences?

The judge had as much experience of criminal cases as he did, more even. Every evening, he took case files home to read in his apartment on Boulevard Saint-Germain, where the light in his study often stayed on until two in the morning.

He had seen men and women of all sorts in the dock and in the witness box.

But wasn't he somewhat aloof from real life? He hadn't gone to the studio in Rue de la Roquette, or to the strange apartment on Boulevard de Charonne. He wasn't familiar with the bustle of those buildings, or with that of the crowded streets, the neighbourhood cafés and dance halls.

Defendants were brought before him between two police officers and everything he knew about them he had gleaned from the pages of a file.

Facts. Sentences. Words. But the rest?

The same applied to his assessors, and to the assistant public prosecutor. The dignity of their office itself set them apart from the rest of the world, and they formed a separate island.

Among the jury, among the public, some were probably better able to understand the character of a man like Meurant, but they had no say in the matter or knew nothing of the complicated workings of the legal system.

As for Maigret, was he not on both sides of the fence at the same time?

'Before allowing you to continue, detective chief inspector, I would like you to tell us the results of the tests on the bloodstains. I am talking about those that were found on the blue suit belonging to the defendant.'

'It is human blood. Forensic analysis subsequently showed that the blood and that of the victim present a sufficient number of similar characteristics for it to be scientifically certain that it is the same blood.'

'Despite that, you carried on with your investigation?'

'Partially because of that, your honour.'

The young lawyer, who had readied himself to challenge Maigret's statement, could not believe his ears and remained on edge while Maigret continued with his reasoning.

'The witness who saw a man in a blue suit and a brown raincoat leave Léontine Faverges' apartment at five o'clock is adamant about the time. Incidentally, that time was also confirmed by the owner of a local shop where that person went before going to her dressmaker in Rue Manuel. If we accept Lombras' testimony, even though he is less certain of the date of his visit to Rue de la Roquette, the defendant was still in his studio at six in the evening, in his grey trousers. We worked out how long it takes to go from the studio to the apartment on Boulevard de Charonne, plus the time to get changed and then to get to Rue Manuel. It would take fifty-five minutes at the very least. The fact that the bank draft presented the next day was not paid also struck me as significant.'

'So you took an interest in Alfred Meurant, the defendant's brother!'

'Yes, your honour. My colleagues and I also investigated other leads.'

'Before authorizing you to let us know the outcome, I must be assured that those leads are closely linked to the case in hand.'

'They are, your honour. For several weeks, inspectors from the Hotel Agency visited a large number of lodging houses in Paris and showed certain photographs.'

'What photographs?'

'Alfred Meurant's, first of all, and then Ginette Meurant's.'

Now it was the defendant who jumped up, outraged, and his lawyer had to get up to calm him and make him sit down again.

'Tell us your conclusions as briefly as possible.'

'Alfred Meurant, the defendant's brother, is well known in some districts, especially around Place des Ternes and Porte Saint-Denis. We found hotel records for him in a little establishment in Rue de l'Étoile where he stayed on several occasions, but there is no evidence that he came to Paris after 1 January.

'And then, although he has been seen with a lot of women, no one remembers noticing him in the company of his sister-in-law, other than more than two years ago.'

Maigret felt Meurant's hostile gaze on him. The defendant had clenched both fists and his lawyer kept turning towards him for fear of an outburst.

'Go on.'

'The photograph of Ginette Meurant was immediately recognized, not only by cinema staff, especially in the neighbourhood, but also in the dance halls, both in Rue de Lappe and around La Chapelle. She frequented these places for several years, always in the afternoons, most recently the one in Rue des Gravilliers.'

'Did she go to them alone?'

'She had a string of male friends, never for long. However, in the months leading up to the murder, she was barely seen.'

Did not these testimonies explain the ambiance of

Boulevard de Charonne, the magazines and the records, their contrast with the books that Meurant bought from the second-hand bookstalls?

'When I went on holiday, just over a month ago,' Maigret went on, 'the Police Judiciaire had not discovered anything further.'

'During this investigation, was Madame Meurant put under police surveillance?'

'Not round the clock, in that she wasn't followed each time she went out and there wasn't always an officer on her doorstep at night.'

Laughter in the courtroom. A disapproving glance from the judge. Silence once again. Maigret mopped his brow, hindered by the hat he was still holding.

'Was this surveillance, albeit sporadic,' asked the judge, not without sarcasm, 'prompted by the letter the defendant sent you from prison, and was it intended to protect his wife?'

'I wouldn't say that.'

'If I understand correctly, you were seeking to find out whom she frequented?'

'Firstly, I wanted to know whether she sometimes met her brother-in-law in secret. Then, not finding any evidence that she did, I started wondering what company she kept and how she spent her time.'

'One more question, detective chief inspector. You interrogated Ginette Meurant at the Police Judiciaire. She stated, if my memory serves me well, that she returned home on 27 February at around eight o'clock in the evening and found dinner about to be served. Did she tell you which suit her husband was wearing?'

'Grey trousers. He wasn't wearing a jacket.'

'And when he'd left her after lunch?'

'He was wearing a grey suit.'

'What time did she leave the apartment on Boulevard de Charonne?'

'At around four.'

'So Meurant could have come home and changed his clothes, then gone out again and put his other suit back on when he returned without her knowing?'

'It is physically possible.'

'Let us go back to the additional investigation you carried out.'

'Surveillance of Ginette Meurant yielded nothing. Since her husband has been in prison, she has stayed at home most of the time, only going out to buy food, visit the prison and, two or three times a week, a trip to the cinema. This surveillance, as I said, was not round the clock. It was occasional. Even so, the results confirm what the neighbours and shopkeepers told us. I returned from holiday the day before yesterday and found a report on my desk. Perhaps it is useful to explain that in the police we never give up on a case altogether, so an arrest is sometimes made unexpectedly, two or three years after the crime or offence.'

'In other words, over the past months, you were no longer *systematically* investigating Ginette Meurant's comings and goings.'

'That is correct. Even so, the inspectors from the Hotel Agency and the Vice Squad, as well as my own inspectors, all had her photograph in their pocket, and that of her brother-in-law. From time to time they would show it. That was how, on 26 September, a witness recognized the young woman in the photograph as being one of his regular customers.'

Meurant became agitated again, and the judge gave him a reprimanding look. Someone in the courtroom protested, probably Ginette Meurant.

'That witness is Nicolas Cajou, manager of a lodging house in Rue Victor-Massé, a stone's throw from Place Pigalle. He usually stays in the office of his establishment, keeping an eye on the comings and goings through the glass door.'

'Was he not questioned last March or in April, like the other landlords?'

'He was in hospital at the time having an operation, and his sister-in-law was minding the place. After that he spent three months convalescing in the Morvan, where he was born, and it was only at the end of September that an officer from the Hotel Agency showed him the photograph on the off chance.'

'The photograph of Ginette Meurant?'

'Yes. He identified her at once, saying that up until he had gone into hospital, she used to come accompanied by a man he did not know. One of the chambermaids, Geneviève Lavancher, also recognized the woman in the photograph.'

The journalists exchanged glances, then looked at the judge in surprise.

'I presume that the companion you are referring to is not Alfred Meurant?'

'No, your honour. Yesterday, in my office, where I'd

summoned Nicolas Cajou and the chambermaid, I showed them several hundred mugshots to confirm that Ginette Meurant's companion was not someone on our files. The man is described as short and stocky with very dark hair. He is elegantly dressed and wears a ring with a yellow stone. He appears to be around thirty years of age and chain-smokes American cigarettes. After each of his visits to Rue Victor-Massé the chambermaid found an ashtray full of cigarette butts, only a few of which were stained with lipstick.

'I didn't have the time, before the trial, to undertake a thorough investigation. Nicolas Cajou was admitted to hospital on 26 February. On the 25th he was still in his office and he states that the couple visited on that day.'

There was a flurry in the courtroom, which Maigret was still unable to see, and the judge raised his voice, a rare occurrence, to say:

'Silence, or I'll clear the court.'

A woman's voice tried to make itself heard:

'Your honour, I—'

'Silence!'

Meurant, his jaws clenched, glared daggers at Maigret.

3.

No one moved while the judge leaned over to confer in hushed tones with his assessors. At one point the red-robed assistant public prosecutor left his seat to join the discussion and shortly afterwards the young counsel for the defence made to do likewise. He visibly hesitated, anxious, not yet assured enough, and was almost on his feet when Judge Bernerie brought down his gavel and all the lawyers went back to their seats as in a tableau.

Xavier Bernerie intoned grudgingly:

'The court thanks the witness for his statement and requests that he does not leave the building.'

Still like a celebrant, he groped around for his judge's cap, picked it up and, rising, concluded his response:

'The hearing is suspended for a quarter of an hour.'

Within seconds, the room sounded like a school playground, erupting in a barely muffled uproar. Half of the spectators left their seats, some stood gesticulating in the aisles, while others pushed and shoved their way to the main door, which the guards had just opened. Meanwhile police officers smuggled the defendant out through an exit concealed in the wood panelling. Pierre Duché tried to fight his way after them, while the jury on the other side of the room also disappeared behind the scenes.

Gowned lawyers, most of them young, including a

woman lawyer who looked like a magazine cover girl, formed a black and white gaggle by the witnesses' entrance. They were discussing articles 310, 311, 312 and the rest of the Code of Criminal Procedure and some spoke excitedly about irregularities in the proceedings that would inevitably result in the case being referred to the Appeal Court.

An elderly lawyer with nicotine-stained teeth, a shiny gown and an unlit cigarette dangling from his lower lip calmly invoked legal precedents, citing two cases, one in Limoges in 1885, the other in Poitiers in 1923, where not only had the preliminary investigation had to go back to square one after the public hearing but it had also taken a different direction as the result of an unanticipated testimony.

Maigret, standing stock still, caught fleeting images and heard snatches of all this, and only had time to identify two of his men in the courtroom through gaps in the crowd before he was besieged by the press.

There was the same buzz as at the theatre, after the first act of a full dress-rehearsal.

'What do you have to say about the bombshell you just dropped, inspector?'

'What bombshell?'

He filled his pipe methodically and felt in need of a drink.

'Do you think Meurant is innocent?'

'I don't think anything.'

'Do you suspect his wife?'

'Forgive me, gentlemen, but I have nothing to add to what I said in the witness box.'

The mob left him in peace all of a sudden because a young reporter had raced over to Ginette Meurant as she battled her way out and the others were afraid of missing a sensational statement.

Everyone watched the moving group. Maigret took advantage of the diversion to slip out of the witnesses' exit. In the corridor he found some men smoking cigarettes, and others who were unfamiliar with the place looking for the urinals.

He knew that the magistrates were deliberating in the judge's chambers and he saw a clerk show in the young Duché, who had been summoned.

It was nearly midday. Bernerie clearly wished to finish with the incident that had arisen during the morning hearing so as to resume the regular course of proceedings in the afternoon, hoping for a verdict that same day.

Maigret reached the gallery and finally lit his pipe. He signalled to Lapointe, whom he'd spotted leaning against a pillar.

He wasn't the only one wanting to take advantage of the adjournment to have a beer. There were people outside, their collars upturned, dashing across the road in the rain to dive into the nearby cafés.

In the refreshment room of the Palais de Justice, an impatient throng in a hurry disturbed the lawyers and their clients who had been quietly discussing their cases.

'Beer?' he asked Lapointe.

'If we can, chief.'

They edged forward between the backs and elbows. Maigret signalled to a waiter he had known for twenty years, and a few moments later two frothy beers were passed to him over people's heads.

'Find out where she has lunch and who with, who she talks to, whether she makes any phone calls, and if so, to whom.'

The tide had already turned, and people were hurrying back to their seats. When Maigret reached the courtroom, it was already too late to get to the rows of benches and he had to stay by the side door among the lawyers.

The jury members were back in position, as was the defendant, flanked by his guards, with his lawyer sitting below him. The judge and his entourage entered and took their seats with dignity, conscious, probably, like Maigret, of the changed mood in the courtroom.

Earlier, it had been a matter of a man accused of having slit the throat of his sixty-year-old aunt and of attempting to strangle and then suffocating a four-year-old girl. Was it not natural that there should be an atmosphere of gloom and oppressive gravity?

Now, after the interval, everything was different. Gaston Meurant had been relegated to the background and the double murder itself had become less important. Maigret's testimony had introduced a new element and raised a new problem – questionable, scandalous – and the spectators had eyes only for the young woman. Those sitting in the back rows desperately craned their necks to see her.

That created a buzz of anticipation, and the judge furiously swept the room with his eyes, as if seeking out those causing the disturbance. This lasted for quite some time, and gradually the noise abated, until it died down completely and silence reigned once more.

'I am warning the public that I will not tolerate any disruption and if there is a single incident I will have the court vacated.'

He cleared his throat and murmured a few words into the ears of his assessors.

'In accordance with the discretionary powers given to me and with the agreement of the assistant public prosecutor and the defence counsel, I have decided to call three new witnesses. Two are in the room and the third, Geneviève Lavancher, who has received a telephone summons, will be at this afternoon's hearing. Usher, please call Madame Ginette Meurant.'

The elderly usher went forward across the empty space to meet the young woman sitting in the front row. She stood up, faltered, and then allowed herself to be led to the witness box.

Maigret had interviewed her several times at Quai des Orfèvres. Then he'd had in front of him a vulgarly flirtatious little woman who was sometimes aggressive.

In honour of the court hearing, she had bought herself a black suit, with a calf-length skirt and coat, the only splash of colour being a straw-yellow blouse.

For the occasion too, Maigret was convinced, to create an air of sophistication, she sported a pillbox hat with a veil, which gave her face an air of mystery.

Her attitude was a mixture of girlish innocence and primness as she bowed her head and gazed up at the judge with frightened, docile eyes.

'Is your name Ginette Meurant, maiden name Chenault?'
'Yes, your honour.'

'Speak louder and turn to the gentlemen of the jury. You are twenty-seven years old and you were born in Saint-Sauveur, in the Nièvre? Is that correct?'

'Yes, your honour.'

'Are you the wife of the defendant?'

She replied in the same respectful tone.

'Pursuant to Article 322, your evidence cannot be accepted by the court, but, with the agreement of the prosecution and the defence, the court is allowed to hear you for information purposes.'

She raised her hand as the previous witnesses had done, but he stopped her.

'No! You are not allowed to take the oath.'

Maigret glimpsed Gaston Meurant's pale face between two others. Chin in his hands, he stared straight ahead of him. From time to time, he clenched his jaws so hard his face bulged.

His wife avoided turning towards him, as if it were forbidden, keeping her eyes riveted on the judge.

'Did you know the victim, Léontine Faverges?'

She appeared hesitant, then mumbled:

'Not very well.'

'What do you mean?'

'That she and I didn't see one another.'

'But you had met her?'

'Once, before we got married. My fiancé insisted on introducing me to her, saying she was his only family.'

'So you went to Rue Manuel?'

'Yes. In the afternoon, at around five o'clock. She gave us hot chocolate and biscuits. I immediately had the feeling she didn't like me and that she'd advise Gaston not to marry me.'

'For what reason?'

She shrugged, cast around for her words, and finally blurted out:

'We weren't the same kind of people.'

A stern look from the judge stemmed the rising laughter.

'Did she not attend your wedding?'

'Yes, she did.'

'What about Alfred Meurant, your brother-in-law?'

'He came too. At that time, he lived in Paris and hadn't yet fallen out with my husband.'

'What was his profession?'

'Sales representative.'

'Did he have regular employment?'

'How would I know? He gave us a coffee service as a wedding present.'

'And did you ever see Léontine Faverges again?'

'Four or five times.'

'Did she come to your home?'

'No. We went to her place. I didn't want to, because I hate imposing on people who don't like me, but Gaston said I had no choice.'

'Why?'

'I don't know.'

'Was it because of her money, by any chance?'

'Maybe.'

'When did you stop visiting Rue Manuel?'

'A long time ago.'

'Two years? Three? Four years?'

'Let's say three years.'

'So you knew about the Chinese vase that was in the sitting room?'

'I have seen it and I even said to Gaston that artificial flowers were only good for funeral wreaths.'

'Did you know what was in the vase?'

'I only knew about the flowers.'

'Your husband never said anything to you?'

'About what? The vase?'

'Gold coins.'

For the first time, she turned towards the dock.

'No.'

'And he didn't tell you either that his aunt kept her money in her apartment instead of depositing it in the bank?'

'I don't remember.'

'You're not certain?'

'Yes I am . . . Yes . . .'

'At the time when you still visited Rue Manuel, albeit not very often, was little Cécile Perrin already living there?'

'I've never seen her. No. She'd have been too young.'

'Did you ever hear your husband speak of her?'

'He must have mentioned her. Wait! Now I'm certain. I was even amazed that a child had been entrusted to a woman like her.'

'Did you know that the defendant used to go and ask his aunt for money quite regularly?'

'He didn't always tell me.'

'But you knew in a general way?'

'I knew that he wasn't a very good businessman, that he got conned by everyone, like when we opened a restaurant in Rue du Chemin-Vert, which could have done very well.'

'What was your job in the restaurant?'

'I served the customers.'

'What about your husband?'

'He worked in the kitchen, helped by an elderly woman.'

'Did he know how to cook?'

'He used a book.'

'Were you alone in the restaurant with the customers?'

'At first, we had a young waitress.'

'When things began to go downhill, did not Léontine Faverges help keep the creditors at bay?'

'I suppose so. I think we still owe money.'

'Did your husband seem anxious during the last few days of February?'

'He was always anxious.'

'Did he talk to you about a bank draft due on the 28th?'

'I didn't pay attention. There were drafts every month.'

'And he didn't tell you that he was going to see his aunt to ask her to help him out once again?'

'I don't remember.'

'Wouldn't that have struck you?'

'No. I was used to it.'

'After the restaurant was closed down, you didn't offer to work?'

'I kept offering, but Gaston didn't want me to.'

'Why not?'

'Maybe because he was jealous.'

'Did he make jealous scenes?'

'Not scenes.'

'Face the gentlemen of the jury.'

'I was forgetting. I'm sorry.'

'On what basis do you claim he was jealous?'

'First of all, he didn't want me to work. Then, at Rue du Chemin-Vert, he would keep popping out of the kitchen to spy on me.'

'Did he ever follow you?'

Pierre Duché fidgeted on his bench, unable to see what the judge was leading up to.

'I didn't notice.'

'In the evenings, did he ask you how you'd spent your day?'

'Yes.'

'What did you tell him?'

'That I'd been to the cinema.'

'Are you sure that you talked to no one about Rue Manuel and Léontine Faverges?'

'Only to my husband.'

'Not to a woman friend?'

'I don't have any women friends.'

'Who did you and your husband socialize with?'

'No one.'

If she was troubled by these questions, she didn't lose her composure.

'Do you remember the suit your husband was wearing at lunchtime on 27 February?'

'His grey suit. It was his weekday one. He only wore the other one on Saturday nights, if we went out, and on Sundays.'

'And to go and see his aunt?'

'Sometimes I think he put on his blue suit.'

'Did he on that day?'

'I wouldn't know. I wasn't at home.'

'You don't know whether he came back to the apartment at some point during the afternoon?'

'How would I know? I was at the cinema.'

'Thank you.'

She stood there, confused, unable to believe that it was over, that she wasn't going to be asked the questions that everyone was expecting.

'You may go back to your seat.'

And the judge continued:

'Bring forward Nicolas Cajou.'

There was a sense of disappointment. The public felt cheated that they had been deprived of a scene to which they were entitled. Ginette Meurant sat down again as if with regret, and a lawyer close to Maigret whispered to his colleagues:

'Lamblin got his hooks into her in the corridor during the adjournment . . .'

Maître Lamblin, whose silhouette resembled that of a starving dog, was the subject of a great deal of gossip at the law courts, rarely complimentary, and had almost been suspended from the bar several times. As if by chance, he was sitting next to the young woman and whispering to her in a congratulatory manner.

The man walking towards the witness box dragging his foot was an entirely different species of humanity. Whereas beneath her make-up Ginette Meurant had the pallor of women who live in hothouses, he, on the other hand, was pasty-faced and made of soft, unhealthy stuff.

Had he grown so thin as a result of his operation? In any case, his clothes were much too big and flapped around his body, which seemed drained of all energy and suppleness.

It was easier to imagine him in his slippers, huddled in the frosted-glass office of his establishment, than walking in the streets of the city.

He had bags under his eyes, folds of skin under his chin.

'Nicolas Cajou, aged sixty-two. You were born in Marillac, in the Cantal, and your profession is manager of a lodging house in Rue Victor-Massé, Paris?'

'Yes, your honour.'

'You are neither a relative nor a friend, nor are you employed by the defendant . . . You swear to tell the truth, the whole truth and nothing but the truth . . . Raise your right hand . . . Say: I swear . . .'

'I swear . . .'

An assessor leaned towards the judge to make an observation, which must have been pertinent because Bernerie seemed struck by it. He thought for a while, and eventually shrugged. Maigret, who had missed nothing of the scene, thought he knew what it meant.

Witnesses who have previous convictions entailing loss of civil rights or who engage in immoral activities are not allowed to take the oath. Now, did not the owner of the lodging house carry out immoral activities, since he accepted in his establishment couples under conditions prohibited by the law? Was it certain that he did not have a criminal record?

It was too late to check, and the judge cleared his throat before asking in a neutral tone:

'Do you keep an up-to-date register of the clients to whom you rent out rooms?'

'Yes, your honour.'

'*All* the clients?'

'All those who spend the night in my hotel.'

'But you don't register the names of those who only stay for a few hours during the daytime?'

'No, your honour. The police will be able to tell you that . . .'

That he was above-board, of course, that there had never been any scandal in his establishment, and that every so often he provided the Hotel Agency or the Vice Squad with vital tip-offs.

'Did you look closely at the witness who was before you on the stand?'

'Yes, your honour.'

'Did you recognize her?'

'Yes, your honour.'

'Tell the gentlemen of the jury in what circumstances you saw this young woman previously.'

'In the usual circumstances.'

One look from Judge Bernerie stifled the laughter.

'In other words?'

'In other words, she often used to come in the afternoon, in the company of a gentleman who rented a room.'

'What do you mean by often?'

'Several times a week.'

'How many, for example?'

'Three or four times.'

'Was she always with the same companion?'

'Yes, your honour.'

'Would you recognize him?'

'Definitely.'

'When was the last time you saw her?'

'The day before I went into hospital, that is 25 February. I remember the date because of my operation.'

'Describe him.'

'Not tall . . . On the short side . . . I suspect that like some men who suffer from being small, he wore special shoes . . . Always well dressed, I'd even say dressed to the nines . . . In our neighbourhood, we know that type . . . It's even the thing that surprised me . . .'

'Why?'

'Because those gentlemen aren't generally in the habit of spending the afternoon in a hotel, especially with the same woman . . .'

'I suppose you know the Montmartre locals pretty much by sight?'

'I'm sorry?'

'I mean the men you're talking about . . .'

'I see them go past.'

'But you have never seen that man anywhere but in your establishment?'

'No, your honour.'

'And you've not heard of him either?'

'I only know that people call him Pierrot.'

'How do you know that?'

'Because sometimes the lady called him Pierrot in front of me.'

'Did he have an accent?'

'Not really. But I always thought he was from the south, or that maybe he was Corsican.'

'Thank you.'

Again, this time, disappointment was on people's faces. They had been expecting a dramatic confrontation and nothing was happening, other than a seemingly innocent series of questions and answers.

The judge looked at the time.

'The hearing is adjourned and will continue at half past two.'

The same din as earlier, only this time the entire courtroom emptied and people thronged to watch Ginette Meurant walk past. It seemed from a distance to Maigret that Maître Lamblin was keeping close behind her and that she turned around every so often to make sure that he was following her.

Maigret had barely stepped outside when he bumped into Janvier, who shot him an inquiring look.

'We've nabbed them, chief. They're both at headquarters.'

It took Maigret a good moment to realize that Janvier was talking about another case, an armed bank robbery in the 20th arrondissement.

'What happened?'

'Lucas arrested them at the home of the mother of one of the boys. The other one was hiding under the bed and the mother didn't know. They hadn't been outside for three days. The poor woman thought her son was ill and was making him hot toddies. She's the widow of a railway worker and she works in a local ironmonger's—'

'How old?'

'The son, eighteen, his friend, twenty.'

'Do they deny it?'

'Yes. But I think you'll catch them out easily.'

'Shall we have lunch together?'

'I warned my wife I wouldn't be home, in any case.'

It was still raining when they crossed Place Dauphine on their way to the brasserie that had become a sort of annexe of the Police Judiciaire.

'And how's it going in court?'

'Nothing definite yet.'

They waited at the bar for a free table.

'I'll have to telephone the judge to request permission to absent myself from the hearing.'

Maigret had no wish to spend the afternoon sitting still among the crowd, in the humid heat, listening to witnesses who from now on would have nothing surprising to contribute. Those witnesses he had questioned in the peace and quiet of his office. And he had visited most of them in their homes, in their habitual surroundings.

Attending court had always been the most painful, most dismal part of his job, and each time he felt the same dread.

Did the court not distort everything? Not through the fault of the judges, juries or witnesses, nor because of the law or the process, but because human beings suddenly found themselves summed up, as it were, in a few phrases, a few sentences.

He sometimes talked about this with his friend Pardon, the neighbourhood doctor, with whom he and his wife were in the habit of having dinner once a month.

One day when his surgery had been relentlessly busy, Pardon had given vent to his disenchantment, if not bitterness.

'Twenty-eight patients this afternoon alone! Barely time to invite them to sit down and ask them a few questions . . . How are you feeling? Where does it hurt? How long has it been going on? . . . The others wait, staring at the baize door, wondering if their turn will ever come . . . Put your tongue out! Get undressed! . . . In most cases, an hour wouldn't be long enough to find out everything I need to know. Each patient is a unique case, and yet I have to work on a production line . . .'

Maigret had then talked to him about the ultimate aim of his own work, in other words the courts, since that is where most investigations culminate.

'Historians,' he'd said, 'learned scholars, spend their lives studying a character from the past, about whom there are already countless books. They go from library to library, archive to archive, looking for the briefest of letters in the hope of getting a little closer to the truth.

'People have been analysing Stendhal's correspondence for over fifty years so as better to understand his personality . . .'

'Is a crime almost always committed by a person who's out of the ordinary? By that I mean someone who's harder to comprehend than the man in the street? I'm given a few weeks, if not days, to enter a new world, to question ten, twenty, fifty people about whom I knew nothing until that day, and to distinguish if possible between the true and the false.

'I'm criticized for going to the scene in person instead of sending my men. On the other hand, it's a miracle that I still have that privilege!

'The examining magistrate who handles the case after me now almost never has that opportunity and only sees people removed from their personal lives, in the neutral surroundings of his chambers.

'In short, what he has in front of him are brush-stroke figures.

'He too only has a limited amount of time; hounded by the press, by public opinion, hampered by a hodge-podge of regulations, swamped by red tape that takes up most of his time, what is he going to find out?

'If they are disembodied creatures when they come out of his chambers, what is left of them by the time they end up in court, and on what will the juries decide the fate of one or several of their kind?

'Now it is no longer a question of months, or weeks, or even days. The number of witnesses is kept to a minimum, likewise the number of questions they are asked.

'They come and repeat in front of the court a condensed version, a digest, as it were, of what they said earlier.

'The case is set out in a few broad outlines, the characters are no more than sketches, if not caricatures . . .'

Had he not had that impression once again that morning while giving his own testimony?

The press would write that he had spoken *at length*, perhaps to their surprise. Any judge other than Xavier Bernerie would certainly not have allowed him more than a few minutes, whereas he had been in the witness box for nearly an hour.

He had endeavoured to be precise, to communicate to those who were listening to him a little of what he felt.

He glanced at the cyclostyled menu and held it out to Janvier.

'I'm going to have the calf's head . . .'

Inspectors stood clustered around the bar. There were two lawyers in the restaurant.

'My wife and I have bought a house, by the way.'

'In the country?'

He had sworn he wouldn't talk about it, not because he liked to be mysterious but out of modesty, because people would be bound to make the connection between this purchase and his retirement, which was not so far off.

'In Meung-sur-Loire?'

'Yes . . . It's like a presbytery . . .'

In two years, there would be no more court appearances for him, other than on the third page of the newspapers. There he would read the testimonies of his successor, Detective Chief Inspector—

But who was going to take his place, in fact? He had no idea. Perhaps they were already beginning to discuss it on high, but of course it was out of the question to mention it in front of him.

'Who do those two kids think they are?'

Janvier shrugged.

'They're all like that nowadays.'

Through the windows, Maigret watched the rain, the grey parapet of the Seine, the cars that had moustaches of dirty water.

'What was the judge like?'

'Very good.'

'What about her?'

'I've instructed Lapointe to tail her. She's fallen into the clutches of a rather dubious lawyer, Lamblin . . .'

'Did she admit to having a lover?'

'She wasn't asked. Bernerie is cautious.'

It was important to remember that it was Gaston Meurant who was on trial, not his wife.

'Did Cajou recognize her?'

'Of course.'

'How did the husband take that?'

'Right then, he would gladly have killed me.'

'Will he be acquitted?'

'It's too soon to tell.'

Steam rose from the plates, smoke from the cigarettes, and the names of the recommended wines were painted in white on the mirrors surrounding the room.

There was a little wine from the Loire, very close to Meung and the house that looked like a presbytery.

4.

At two o'clock, Maigret, with Janvier still in tow, climbed up the main staircase of Quai des Orfèvres, which was always dank and gloomy, even on the most cheerful summer morning. Today a damp draught was blowing and the wet footprints on the steps would not dry.

Already on the first-floor landing they could hear a clamour, then came the sound of voices, comings and goings indicating that the press had been alerted and was there, with the photographers and probably people from the television, if not the cinema.

At the Palais de Justice, one case was coming to a close, or seemed to be, while another was beginning here. At one end of the building, there was already a crowd, at the other, there were only the professionals.

Quai des Orfèvres also had a sort of witnesses' room, the glazed waiting room nicknamed the glass cage, and Maigret paused in passing to glance at the six people sitting beneath the photographs of police officers killed in the line of duty.

Was it possible that all witnesses were alike? This lot belonged to the same world as those at the Palais de Justice, ordinary people, humble workers, and, among them, two women who sat staring straight ahead, their hands resting on their leather bags.

The reporters raced towards Maigret, who raised a hand to subdue them.

'Calm down! Calm down! Don't forget, gentlemen, that I don't know anything yet and that I haven't seen the boys . . .'

He opened the door to his office, promising:

'In two or three hours maybe, if I have any news for you . . .'

He closed the door behind him and said to Janvier:

'Go and see if Lapointe is here yet.'

He slipped back into his old routine from before the holidays, almost a ritual which for him was comparable to the courtroom ceremonial. Removing his coat and hat, he hung them in the cupboard which also contained an enamel basin for him to wash his hands. Then he sat down at his desk and fiddled with his pipes before selecting one and filling it.

Janvier came back with Lapointe.

'I'll see your two blockheads in a few minutes.'

And to the young Lapointe:

'So, what did she do?'

'She was mobbed by a bunch of journalists and photographers who followed her along the corridors and down the main staircase and there were more waiting for her outside. There was even a cinema newsreel bus parked by the kerb. I only glimpsed her face a couple of times. You could tell she was terrified, and I'm told she begged them to leave her in peace.

'All of a sudden, Lamblin barged through the crowd, grabbed her by the arm and pulled her over to a taxi which he'd found in the meantime. He made her get in and the car drove off in the direction of Pont Saint-Michel.

'It was like a conjuring trick. I didn't manage to find a taxi so I couldn't follow them. Just a few minutes ago, Macé, from *Le Figaro,* came back to the Palais de Justice. He was lucky, he had his car nearby and was able to tail the taxi.

'According to him, Maître Lamblin took Ginette Meurant to a restaurant on Place de l'Odéon that specializes in seafood and bouillabaisse. They had a leisurely lunch there, just the two of them.

'Now, everyone's back in the courtroom and they're just waiting for the judge.'

'Go back in there. Telephone me from time to time. I'd like to know whether the chambermaid's testimony causes a stir . . .'

Maigret had managed to get hold of the judge on the phone and had been given permission not to waste his afternoon in court.

The five inspectors scattered among the public that morning had found out nothing. They'd studied the crowd with as keen an eye as the spotters in a casino, but none of the men present corresponded to the description of Ginette Meurant's companion given by Nicolas Cajou. As for Alfred Meurant, the defendant's brother, he wasn't in court, or in Paris, as Maigret already knew after a telephone call from the Toulon Flying Squad.

Two inspectors stayed in the courtroom, just in case, as well as Lapointe, who went back to the neighbouring building via the internal corridors.

Maigret called Lucas, who had been dealing with the bank raid.

'I didn't want to question them before you'd seen them, chief. Earlier, I held an identity parade.'

'Did the witnesses recognize both of them?'

'Yes. Especially the one whose mask had fallen off, of course.'

'Bring in the youngest one.'

His hair was too long, and he had a spotty face. He looked unhealthy and unwashed.

'Remove his handcuffs . . .'

The boy glowered at him warily, determined not to fall into any of the traps they were bound to set him.

'Leave me alone with him.'

In cases like this, Maigret preferred to be on his own with the suspect. There would be plenty of time later to take his statement in writing and have him sign it.

He puffed rapidly on his pipe.

'Sit down.'

He nudged a packet of cigarettes towards the youth.

'Do you smoke?'

The boy's hand was shaking. At the end of his long, square fingers, his nails were bitten like those of a child.

'Is your father still around?'

'It wasn't me.'

'I'm not asking whether it was you who acted the idiot or not. I'm asking you if your father's still around.'

'He's dead.'

'From what?'

'In the sanatorium.'

'Is it your mother who keeps you?'

'I work too.'

'Doing what?'

'I'm a polisher.'

This was going to take some time. Maigret knew from experience that it was better to proceed slowly.

'How did you get hold of the automatic?'

'I haven't got an automatic.'

'Do you want me to bring in the witnesses waiting outside straight away?'

'They're liars.'

The telephone was already ringing. It was Lapointe.

'Geneviève Lavancher has testified, chief. They asked her more or less the same questions as they asked her employer, plus another one. The judge asked her if, on 25 February, she had noticed anything particular about her clients' behaviour and she replied that yes, funnily enough, she was surprised to see that the bed hadn't been disturbed.'

'Are the usual witnesses testifying?'

'Yes, it's all going very quickly. No one's really listening to them.'

It took forty minutes to break down the boy's resistance, and he ended up blubbing.

He was the one who'd been holding the automatic. There had been three, not two of them, because an accomplice had been waiting at the wheel of a stolen car. Allegedly he was the one who'd come up with the idea of the robbery, but then he'd scarpered as soon as he heard the cries for help, without waiting for the others.

Despite that, the kid, whose name was Virieu, refused to give the name of the accomplice.

'Is he older than you?'

'Yes, he's twenty-three and he's married.'

'And was he experienced?'

'So he said.'

'I'll question you again later, when I've talked to your friend.'

Virieu was led away and Giraucourt, his friend, brought in. His handcuffs were also removed, and the two boys managed to exchange looks as they passed each other.

'Did he spill the beans?'

'Were you expecting him to keep quiet?'

Routine. The hold-up had failed. There were no dead or injured, not even any breakages, apart from one windowpane.

'Whose idea were the masks?'

The idea wasn't exactly original. A few months earlier, professionals in Nice had worn carnival masks to attack a mail van.

'You weren't armed?'

'No.'

'It was you who said, when a member of staff moved towards the window: "Shoot, you idiot . . ."'

'I don't know what I said, I lost my head . . .'

'Except that your little friend obeyed and released the catch.'

'He didn't shoot.'

'In other words, it's lucky the shot didn't fire. Maybe

there were no cartridges in the chamber? Maybe the gun was faulty?'

The bank staff and a woman customer put their hands up. It was ten o'clock in the morning.

'It was you who ran in shouting: "Everyone against the wall with your hands in the air. This is a hold-up!"

'And apparently you added: "We're not kidding."'

'I said that because a woman burst out laughing.'

A 45-year-old bank clerk, who was now waiting in the glass cage with the other witnesses, had grabbed a paperweight and thrown it at the window, shouting for help.

'Have you ever been in prison?'

'Once.'

'For what offence?'

'For stealing a camera from a car.'

'Do you know what it's going to cost you, this time?'

The boy shrugged, trying to act tough.

'Five years, young man. As for your friend, whether his weapon jammed or not, it's highly likely that he'll get at least ten years . . .'

It was true. They'd pick up the third boy sooner or later. The investigation would move quickly and since this wasn't a recess period, there would be no delay in bringing the case to court. In three or four months' time, Maigret would once again be called to testify before the court.

'Take him away, Lucas. There's no reason to keep him and his friend apart now. Let the two of them chat as much as they like. Bring me the first witness.'

After that it was just a matter of formalities and

paperwork. And according to Lapointe, who had telephoned, things were moving even faster at the Palais de Justice where some witnesses, after spending only five minutes on the stand, found themselves, perplexed and a little disappointed, trying to squeeze themselves in among the crowd.

At five o'clock, Maigret was still working on the bank-raid case and his office, where the lamps were lit, was thick with pipe smoke.

'The plaintiff has just been allowed to say something. Maître Lioran gave a brief statement. Given the unforeseen developments, he supports in advance the assistant public prosecutor's conclusions.'

'Is the assistant public prosecutor speaking at the moment?'

'He has been for the past two minutes.'

'Call me back as soon as he's finished.'

Half an hour later, Lapointe phoned in a fairly detailed report. In essence Aillevard, the prosecutor, had said:

'We are here to try Gaston Meurant, accused of having, on 27 February, slit the throat of his aunt, Léontine Faverges, then suffocating to death a little girl aged four, Cécile Perrin, whose mother instigated civil proceedings.'

The mother, with dyed auburn hair, still wearing her fur coat, let out a wail and had to be led sobbing from the courtroom.

The assistant public prosecutor went on:

'We have heard some unexpected testimonies from the witness box which we are unable to take into account with regard to this case. The charges against the defendant have not changed and the questions which the jury must answer remain the same.

'Did Gaston Meurant have the material means to commit this double murder and to steal Léontine Faverges' savings?

'It has been established that he knew the secret of the Chinese vase and that on several occasions his aunt took money from it to give him.

'Does he have a sufficient motive?

'The day after the crime, on 28 February, he was to be presented with a bank draft which he had signed but didn't have the necessary funds to pay, and he was on the verge of bankruptcy.

'And lastly, do we have the proof of his presence, the previous afternoon, at Rue Manuel?

'Six days later, a navy-blue suit belonging to him was found in a cupboard in his apartment on Boulevard de Charonne. It had bloodstains on the sleeve and on the lapel for which he could offer no explanation.

'According to the experts, it is human blood and, more than likely, that of Léontine Faverges.

'However, there are testimonies that would seem to be contradictory, despite the good faith of the witnesses.

'Madame Ernie, a client of the victim's neighbour, saw a man wearing a navy-blue suit leave Léontine Faverges' apartment at five o'clock and feels she can swear that this man had very dark brown hair.

'On the other hand, you heard a piano teacher, Monsieur Germain Lombras, tell you that at six that evening he spoke with the defendant in his workshop in Rue de la

Roquette. Monsieur Germain Lombras did however admit to a slight doubt as to the date of this visit.

'We are confronted with a heinous crime, committed in cold blood by a man who not only attacked a defenceless woman but also had no scruples about murdering a child.

'There can therefore be no question of mitigating circumstances but only of the death penalty.

'Now it is up to the jury to say whether in all good conscience, they find Gaston Meurant guilty of this double murder.'

Maigret, who had finished with his amateur gangsters, resigned himself to opening his door and facing the press.

'Did they confess?'

He nodded.

'Not too much publicity please, gentlemen. Above all don't make them sound like heroes! Don't give anyone who might be tempted to follow their example the impression that these kids have pulled off a feat. They're sad cases, believe me . . .'

He answered their questions curtly, feeling heavy and tired. His mind was partly in the courtroom, where it was the turn of the young defence counsel to sum up.

Maigret was tempted to open the glass door that communicated with the Palais de Justice to go and join Lapointe, but what was the use? He imagined the defence speech, which would open in the same way as a trashy novel.

No doubt Pierre Duché would go as far back into the past as possible.

A poor family from Le Havre, teeming with children who had to fend for themselves. From the age of fifteen or sixteen, the girls went into service; in other words they left for Paris, where they were supposed to go into service. Did the parents have the time or means to worry about them? The girls would send a letter home once a month, in laboured handwriting, full of spelling mistakes, sometimes enclosing a postal order for a small sum.

Two sisters left, first Léontine, who was hired as a sales assistant in a department store, and soon married.

Hélène, the younger one, had worked in a dairy, and then in a haberdashery in Rue d'Hauteville.

Léontine's husband died. As for Hélène, it wasn't long before she discovered the local dance halls.

Did the two of them stay in touch? It wasn't certain. After the death of her husband in an accident, Léontine Faverges became a familiar face in the brasseries on Rue Royale and the lodging houses in the Madeleine neighbourhood before setting up on her own in Rue Manuel.

Her sister had two children from unknown fathers and had raised them as best she could for two or three years. Then she had been taken to hospital one evening for an operation from which she never emerged.

'My client, gentlemen of the jury, brought up in care . . .'

It was true, and Maigret could have provided interesting statistics on the subject – for example the percentage of orphans raised in care who went off the rails and ended up in the courts.

They were the ones who rebelled, who bore a grudge against society for their humiliating situation.

But, contrary to general belief and to what the members of the jury doubtless thought, they were the minority.

Many of the others were probably scarred too. Throughout their lives they felt inferior. But their reaction, on the other hand, was to prove to themselves that they were as good as anyone else.

They were taught a profession and they strove to become first-class craftsmen.

Their pride and joy was to establish a family, a proper one, a regular one, with children they took out for a Sunday promenade, holding their hands.

And what sweeter revenge than setting up on their own one day and becoming the boss of a small business?

Had Pierre Duché thought of that? Was that what he was telling them, in the courtroom, where people were beginning to look haggard?

That morning, during the long interrogation he had been subjected to, Maigret had forgotten something, and now he was annoyed with himself. True, the cross-examination was on the record. But it was merely an unimportant detail.

The third time that Ginette Meurant had come to the Police Judiciaire, to his office, Maigret had asked her casually:

'You've never had children?'

The question took her aback and she looked startled.

'Why are you asking me that?'

'I don't know . . . I have the impression that your husband is the sort of man to want a family . . . Am I wrong?'

'No.'

'Did he hope to have children with you?'

'At first, yes.'

He had sensed a hesitation, something like unease, and had probed further.

'You weren't able to have children?'

'No.'

'Did he know that when he married you?'

'No. We'd never talked about that.'

'When did he find out?'

'After a few months. Because he kept hoping and he'd ask me the same question every month, I decided to tell him the truth . . . Not the entire truth . . . But the main thing . . .'

'What do you mean?'

'That I had been ill, before meeting him, and that I'd had an operation . . .'

That had been seven years ago. Whereas Meurant had hoped to have a family, there had been just the two of them.

He had set up his workshop on his own. Then, under pressure from his wife, he had given it up and tried a different profession for a while. Predictably, it had been a disaster. Nevertheless, he had patiently started over again and built up a small picture-framing business.

Maigret believed all these details were connected. Rightly or wrongly, he suddenly attached a great deal of importance to the question of children.

He wouldn't go so far as to claim that Meurant was innocent. He had seen men just as self-effacing, calm and mild-mannered turn violent.

Nearly always in such cases it was because, for one reason or another, they had been wounded deep down inside.

Meurant, driven by jealousy, could have committed a crime of passion. Perhaps he could also have attacked a friend who had humiliated him.

Perhaps too, if his aunt had refused him the money he desperately needed . . .

Anything was possible, except, it seemed to Maigret, for a man who had so longed for a child to deliberately suffocate a little four-year-old girl.

'Hello, chief . . .'

'Yes?'

'He's done. The judge and the jury are retiring. Some people expect it to take a long time, but others are convinced that the die is cast.'

'How is Meurant behaving?'

'All afternoon he acted as though the case didn't concern him. He seemed absent, downcast. When his lawyer spoke to him, on two or three occasions, he merely shrugged. Finally, when the judge asked him whether he wished to make a statement, he appeared not to understand. The judge had to repeat the question. He simply shook his head.'

'Did he look at his wife at all?'

'Not once.'

'Thank you. Now listen carefully: did you spot Bonfils in the courtroom?'

'Yes. He's sitting close to Ginette Meurant.'

'Tell him not to lose sight of her afterwards. To make certain she doesn't throw him off, he should have Jussieu help him. One of them should ensure they have a car waiting.'

'Got it. I'll pass on your orders.'

'She'll end up going home eventually and we need a man outside the building on Boulevard de Charonne around the clock.'

'And what if . . . ?'

'If Meurant's acquitted, I'm sending Janvier over there to take care of him.'

'Do you think that . . . ?'

'I have no idea, my boy.'

It was true. He had done his best. He was seeking the truth, but there was no proof that he had found it, not even partially.

The investigation had taken place in March and early April, with great bursts of sunshine over Paris, light clouds and scattered showers suddenly creating cool, misty mornings.

The procedure was coming to its conclusion in a wet, gloomy early autumn, with a low spongy sky and glistening pavements.

Maigret did some paperwork to kill time, and went and paced around the inspectors' office, issuing instructions to Janvier.

'Make sure you keep me posted, even in the middle of the night.'

Despite his imperturbable air, he was anxious, worried all of a sudden, as if he were annoyed at himself for having taken on too heavy a responsibility.

When the telephone rang in his office, he pounced on it.

'It's over, chief!'

Lapointe's voice was drowned out by various noises, a great uproar.

'There were four questions, two for each of the victims. The answer is no to all four. As I speak, the lawyer's trying to guide Meurant to the clerk's office, despite the crowd that's—'

His words were lost for a moment in the din.

'Sorry, chief . . . I grabbed the first telephone I saw . . . I'll be back in the office as soon as I can.'

Maigret started pacing again, filling his pipe, picking up another one because that one didn't draw, opening and closing his door three times.

The corridors of the Police Judiciaire were deserted once more and in the glass cage there was only one regular, an occasional informer.

When Lapointe arrived, he was still buzzing with the excitement of the court.

'A lot of people expected it, but all the same it created a stir . . . The whole room was on its feet . . . The little girl's mother, who had gone back to her seat, fainted and was almost trampled—'

'What about Meurant?'

'He seemed not to understand. He allowed himself to be led away without really grasping what was happening to him. The reporters who managed to approach him couldn't get a word out of him. Then they turned their attention to his wife, with Lamblin acting as her bodyguard.

'Immediately after the verdict, she tried to rush over to Meurant, as if to throw her arms around his neck . . . He had already turned his back to the room—'

'Where is she?'

'Lamblin took her into some office, near the lawyers' robing room . . . Jussieu's taking care of her . . .'

It was six thirty. The Police Judiciaire was beginning to empty, lights were being switched off.

'I'm going home for dinner.'

'What about me? What should I do?'

'You must eat too, and go to bed.'

'Do you think anything's going to happen?'

Maigret, who was opening the cupboard to take out his overcoat and hat, merely shrugged.

'Do you remember the search?'

'Very well.'

'Are you sure there was no gun in the apartment?'

'Certain. I'm convinced that Meurant has never owned a gun. He didn't even do his military service, because of his eyesight . . .'

'See you tomorrow, then.'

'See you tomorrow, chief.'

Maigret took the bus, then walked down Boulevard Richard-Lenoir, his collar turned up and his shoulders hunched. As he reached the landing of his apartment, the door opened, creating a rectangle of warm light and exuding cooking aromas.

'Happy?' asked Madame Maigret.

'Why?'

'Because he's been acquitted.'

'How do you know?'

'I just heard it on the wireless.'

'What else are they saying?'

'That his wife was waiting for him outside and they got into a taxi to go home.'

Maigret stepped back into his domestic life, put on his slippers and resumed his usual habits.

'Are you very hungry?'

'I don't know. What's for dinner?'

He was thinking about another apartment on Boulevard de Charonne, where there was another couple. There was probably no dinner waiting, but maybe some ham and cheese in the larder.

In the street, two inspectors were pacing up and down in the rain, unless they'd found shelter in a doorway.

What was happening? What had Gaston Meurant, who had been in prison for seven months, said to his wife? How was he looking at her? Had she tried to kiss him, to place her hand over his?

Had she claimed that all the things that had been said about her were untrue? Or was she asking for his forgiveness, swearing that he was the only man she loved?

Would he return to his shop, his picture-framing workshop in the courtyard, the next day?

Maigret ate mechanically and Madame Maigret knew that this was not the time to question him.

The telephone rang.

'Hello, yes . . . Speaking . . . Vacher? . . . Is Jussieu still with you?'

'I'm calling from a local café to update you . . . I've nothing special to report, but I thought you'd like to know—'

'Did they go home?'

'Yes.'

'Alone?'

'Yes. A few moments later, the lights on the third floor went on. I saw shadows coming and going behind the curtains.'

'What next?'

'After around half an hour, the wife came down, holding an umbrella. Jussieu followed her. She didn't go far, only into a charcuterie and a bakery, and then she went back up to her apartment—'

'Did Jussieu see her from close up?'

'Fairly close, through the window of the charcuterie.'

'How did she seem?'

'She looked as if she'd been crying. Her cheeks were red, her eyes shiny—'

'Did she not appear anxious?'

'Jussieu says she didn't.'

'And since?'

'I imagine they ate. I saw Ginette Meurant's shape in what appears to be the bedroom—'

'Is that all?'

'Yes. Should we both stay here?'

'It's best. I'd like one of you to keep watch inside the building later. The residents probably go to bed early.

Jussieu could stand guard on the landing, for example, once the comings and goings have stopped. He can let the concierge know and ask her to keep quiet about it.'

'Very well, chief.'

'Call me back in two hours in any case.'

'If the café's still open.'

'Otherwise, I may drop by.'

There was no gun in the apartment, true, but hadn't Léontine Faverges' murderer used a knife, which, incidentally, had never been found? A very sharp knife, according to the experts, who thought it was probably a butcher's knife.

All the cutlers and ironmongers in Paris had been questioned, but of course to no avail.

When all was said and done, the only definite fact was that a woman and a little girl were dead, that a certain bloodstained blue suit belonged to Gaston Meurant and that his wife, at the time of the murder, was in the habit of meeting a lover several times a week in a furnished room in Rue Victor-Massé.

That was all, and the jury had just acquitted the picture-framer due to lack of evidence.

Although there was no conclusive proof of his guilt, there was no conclusive proof of his innocence either.

During her husband's incarceration, Ginette Meurant had led an exemplary life, barely leaving her apartment and not meeting any dubious individuals.

There was no telephone in her apartment. Her post had been opened but had yielded nothing.

'Are you really planning to go over there tonight?'

'I'll just drop in before I go to bed.'

'Are you afraid something will happen?'

What could he say? That the two of them were ill-suited to live together in the bizarre apartment where *History of the Consulate and the Empire* sat side-by-side with silk dolls and confessions of film stars on the shelves of the cosy-corner.

5.

At around eleven thirty in the evening, Maigret alighted from a taxi on Boulevard de Charonne. Jussieu emerged noiselessly from the shadows, his face wearing the blank expression of an officer on night surveillance. He pointed to a lit window above them, on the third floor. It was one of the few lights on in the neighbourhood – a neighbourhood where people left early in the morning to go to work.

The rain was beginning to ease up and there were glimmers of silvery moonlight between the clouds.

'That window's the dining room,' explained Jussieu, who reeked of cigarettes. 'The bedroom light went off half an hour ago.'

Maigret waited for a few minutes, hoping to catch signs of activity behind the curtain. Since there was no movement, he went home to bed.

The next day, from the reports and telephone calls, he would reconstruct and follow the Meurants' movements hour by hour.

At six o'clock in the morning, as the concierge was bringing in the rubbish bins, two inspectors arrived to relieve Vacher and Jussieu, but they didn't go inside the building because it was no longer possible for one of them to lurk on the stairs during the daytime.

The report given by Vacher, who had spent the night either sitting on a stair or standing outside the door as soon as he heard any sound inside the apartment, was somewhat disturbing.

Quite early, after a meal during which the couple had barely spoken, Ginette Meurant went into the bedroom to get undressed; Jussieu, who had watched her shadow from the street, confirmed he had seen her slip her dress over her head.

Her husband had not followed her. She went to say a few words to him, and had apparently gone to bed while he stayed sitting in an armchair in the dining room.

Then, several times, he'd stood up and paced up and down, pausing occasionally, resuming his pacing, and then sitting down.

At around midnight, his wife had come to talk to him again. From the landing, Vacher hadn't been able to hear what they were saying, but he could make out the two voices. They didn't sound as if they were arguing. It was a sort of monologue by the wife, punctuated, from time to time, by a curt phrase or even a single word from the husband.

She had gone back to bed, still alone, apparently. The dining-room light had stayed on and, at around two thirty, Ginette was back again. Meurant hadn't been asleep, because he replied straight away, brusquely. Vacher thought she'd been crying. He'd heard a continual whimpering interspersed with tell-tale sniffling.

Again without anger, the husband had sent her back to

bed and had probably ended up falling asleep in his armchair.

Later, a baby had woken up on the floor above; there had been muffled footsteps and then, from five o'clock onwards, the residents had begun to rise. Lights had come on and the aroma of coffee filled the stairwell. Already at five thirty, one man left for work, darting an inquisitive glance at the inspector who had nowhere to hide, then he looked at the door and seemed to grasp what was going on.

Dupeu and Baron took over outside at six. The rain had stopped, and water was dripping from the trees. The fog made it impossible to see further than twenty metres away.

The dining-room light was still on, the bedroom one was off. Meurant soon came out, unshaven, his clothes crumpled as if he'd slept in them. He headed towards the bar-tobacconist's on the corner where he drank three cups of black coffee and ate croissants. As he was about to open the door to leave, he changed his mind and went back to the bar where he ordered a brandy, which he downed in one.

The investigation carried out in the spring had indicated that he wasn't a drinker, that he drank barely one glass of wine with his meals and, in summer, just the occasional beer.

He made his way on foot to Rue de la Roquette, without looking behind him to see whether he was being followed. On reaching his shop, he paused for a moment in front of the closed shutters but did not go in. He continued into the courtyard and unlocked the door of the glass-fronted studio.

He stood there for a long time, doing nothing, looking about him at the work table, the tools on hooks on the walls, the suspended frames, the planks of wood and the shavings. Water had seeped under the door and formed a little puddle on the concrete floor.

Meurant opened the stove door and put in some kindling and leftover lumps of coal, then, about to strike a match, he changed his mind, left the workshop and locked the door behind him.

He walked for quite a while, as if with no particular destination in mind. At Place de la République, he went into another bar where he drank a second brandy while the waiter stared at him as if wondering where he'd seen his face before.

Did he realize? A couple of passers-by had also turned around to look at him because that morning his photograph had appeared in the newspapers again under the headline:

GASTON MEURANT ACQUITTED

That headline and photo were in all the kiosks, but he wasn't curious enough to buy a paper. He took the bus, got off twenty minutes later at Place Pigalle and headed for Rue Victor-Massé.

At last he came to the furnished lodgings owned by Nicolas Cajou, the Hôtel du Lion, and stood gazing at the façade for a long time.

When he set off again, it was to go back down in the direction of the Grands Boulevards. He walked unsteadily, pausing sometimes at a junction as if he didn't know which way to go, and stopping at one point to buy a packet of cigarettes.

He went down Rue Montmartre to Les Halles and the inspector tailing him almost lost him in the crowd. At Châtelet, he drank a third brandy, again downing it in one, and at last he reached Quai des Orfèvres.

Now it was daylight, the yellowish fog was less dense. Maigret, in his office, was taking a telephone report from Dupeu, who had remained on surveillance outside the Meurants' apartment in Boulevard de Charonne.

'The wife got up at seven fifty. I saw her draw the curtains and open the window to look out into the street as if searching for her husband. She probably hadn't heard him leave and was surprised to find the dining room empty. I think she spotted me, chief . . .'

'It doesn't matter. If she goes out too, try not to let her give you the slip.'

Gaston Meurant stood dithering outside on Quai des Orfèvres, gazing up at the windows of the Police Judiciaire in the same way he had looked at those of the furnished lodging house. It was 9.30. He continued on to Pont Saint-Michel, was about to cross the bridge but then retraced his steps and, marching past the officer on guard, walked through the entrance to the building.

He was familiar with the place. He was seen slowly mounting the grey stairs, stopping, not to catch his breath but because he was still undecided.

'He's on his way up, chief!' Baron telephoned from his room on the ground floor.

And Maigret repeated to Janvier, who was in his office: 'He's coming up.'

They both waited. Meurant took an age. He couldn't make up his mind but skulked in the corridor, stopping outside Maigret's door as if he was going to knock unannounced.

'What do you want?' asked Joseph, the elderly clerk.

'I'd like to speak to Detective Chief Inspector Maigret.'

'This way please. Fill in the form.'

Pencil in hand, he was still thinking of leaving when Janvier came out of Maigret's office.

'Have you come to see Detective Chief Inspector Maigret? Follow me.'

For Meurant, all this must have felt like a nightmare. He looked as if he'd barely slept, his eyes were bloodshot, and he smelled of cigarettes and alcohol. But he wasn't drunk. He followed Janvier, who opened the door, showed him into the room and closed it without going in himself.

Maigret, at his desk, appeared to be engrossed in a file. He didn't raise his eyes immediately but then turned to his visitor, without showing any surprise, and muttered:

'Just a moment . . .'

He annotated a document, then another, mumbling distractedly:

'Have a seat.'

Meurant did not sit down, did not venture further into the room. His patience running out, he said:

'You imagine perhaps that I've come to say thank you?'

His voice was not entirely natural. He sounded a little hoarse and was trying to introduce a note of sarcasm.

'Have a seat,' repeated Maigret without looking at him.

This time, Meurant took three steps forward and grabbed the back of a chair with a green velvet seat.

'Did you do that to save me?'

At last, Maigret looked him up and down, calmly.

'You look tired, Meurant.'

'This is not about me but about what you did yesterday.'

His voice was fainter, as if he'd been trying hard to contain his anger.

'I have come to tell you that I don't believe you, that you lied, as those people lied, that I'd rather be in prison, that you have acted wrongly . . .'

Had the alcohol made him lose his grip on reality? Possibly. But, once again, he wasn't drunk and he must have been saying those words over and over to himself for most of the night.

'Have a seat.'

At last! He made up his mind, reluctantly, as if he sensed a trap.

'You may smoke.'

In protest, much as he wanted to, he refrained, so as not to be beholden to Maigret. His hand was trembling.

'It is easy to say anything you want to people like that, who are reliant on the police . . .'

He clearly meant Nicolas Cajou, the lodging-house manager, and the chambermaid.

Maigret lit his pipe, slowly, and waited.

'You know as well as I do that it's not true . . .'

His anguish caused beads of sweat to form on his forehead. Maigret finally spoke.

'You claim that you killed your aunt and little Cécile Perrin?'

'You know I didn't.'

'I don't *know*, but I am convinced you didn't do it. Why is that, do you think?'

Surprised, Meurant was at a loss to answer.

'There are a lot of children in your apartment building in Boulevard de Charonne, aren't there?'

Meurant said yes, automatically.

'You hear them coming in and going out. Sometimes, after school, they play on the stairs. Do you talk to them occasionally?'

'I know them.'

'Even though you don't have children yourself, you know the school timetable. That struck me from the start of the investigation. Cécile Perrin went to nursery school. Léontine Faverges would go and pick her up at four o'clock every day, except Thursday. So until four o'clock, your aunt was alone in the apartment.'

Meurant tried to follow his drift.

'You had a large payment due on 28 February, true. It is possible that the last time you borrowed money from her, Léontine Faverges had said to you that she would not let you have any more. Supposing you had planned to kill her to take the money from the Chinese vase and the shares . . .'

'I didn't kill her.'

'Let me finish. I was saying: supposing that had been your plan, you had no reason to go to Rue Manuel after four o'clock and, consequently, to have to kill two people instead of one. Criminals who needlessly attack children are rare and belong to a well-defined category.'

Meurant, whose eyes had misted over, looked as if he was about to cry.

'The person who murdered Léontine Faverges and the child was either unaware of the little girl's existence or had to strike in the late afternoon. Now, if he knew the secret of the vase and the drawer containing the shares, he was probably also aware of Cécile Perrin's presence in the apartment.'

'What are you getting at?'

'Have a cigarette.'

The man obeyed mechanically, continuing to gaze at Maigret with suspicion, but there was less anger in his eyes.

'We're still speculating, aren't we? The murderer knows that you are to come to Rue Manuel at six o'clock. He knows that in most cases the forensic pathologists – the newspapers have repeated it often enough – are able to determine the time of death to within one or two hours.'

'No one knew that . . .'

His voice had changed and now he looked away from Maigret's face.

'By committing his crime at around five o'clock, the murderer was almost certain that you would come under suspicion. He could not foresee that a customer would turn up at your workshop at six o'clock and, besides, the music teacher was unable to give a formal statement because he wasn't sure of the date.'

'No one knew . . .' repeated Meurant mechanically.

Maigret abruptly changed the subject.

'Do you know your neighbours at Boulevard de Charonne?'

'I say hello to them in passing.'

'They never come to your apartment, not even for a cup of coffee? You never go into theirs? You aren't on friendly terms with any of them?'

'No.'

'So the chances are they have never heard of your aunt.'

'Now they have!'

'But not before. Did you and your wife have a lot of friends in Paris?'

Meurant replied unwillingly, as if he were afraid that if he gave way on one point, he would have to do so all the way down the line.

'What difference does it make?'

'Who did you go and have dinner with occasionally?'

'No one.'

'Who did you go on Sunday outings with?'

'With my wife.'

'And she has no family in Paris. Neither do you, apart from your brother, who spends most of his time in the south and with whom you haven't been on speaking terms for the last two years.'

'We didn't fall out.'

'But you stopped seeing him.'

And once again, Maigret appeared to change the subject.

'How many keys are there to your apartment?'

'Two. My wife has one and I have the other.'

'And it never happened that, when you went out, one of you left the key with the concierge or a neighbour?'

Aware that Maigret never said anything without good reason, Meurant chose to say nothing, even though he was unable to see where all this was leading.

'The lock wasn't forced that day, as the experts who examined it confirmed. And yet, if you didn't kill them, someone got into your apartment twice, the first time to take your blue suit out of the bedroom wardrobe and the second to put it back so carefully that you didn't notice anything. Do you admit that?'

'I admit nothing. All I know is that my wife . . .'

'When you met her, seven years ago, you were a loner. Am I mistaken?'

'I worked all day, and in the evenings I'd read, and occasionally I went to the cinema.'

'Did she throw herself at you?'

'No.'

'Didn't other men, other customers at the restaurant where she was a waitress, chase after her?'

He clenched his fists.

'So what if they did?'

'How long did you have to keep asking before she agreed to go out with you?'

'Three weeks.'

'What did you do, that first evening?'

'We went to the cinema, and then she wanted to go dancing.'

'Are you a good dancer?'

'No.'

'Did she make fun of you?'

Increasingly disconcerted by the turn the conversation was taking, he said nothing.

'Did you take her back to your place afterwards?'

'No.'

'Why not?'

'Because I loved her.'

'What about the second time?'

'We went to the cinema again.'

'And then?'

'To a hotel.'

'Why not to your place?'

'Because I was living in a shabby room at the back of a courtyard.'

'You already intended to marry her, and you were afraid she'd be put off?'

'I wanted to make her my wife right away.'

'Did you know that she had a lot of male friends?'

'That's no one else's business. She was free.'

'Did you tell her about your profession, your shop? Because you already had a shop, in Faubourg Saint-Antoine, unless I'm mistaken.'

'Of course I told her about it.'

'Was it not with the idea of enticing her? On marrying you she'd become the wife of a shopkeeper.'

Meurant turned red.

'Do you realize now that you were the one who wanted to have her, and that to win her, you were not averse to cheating a little. Did you have any debts?'

'No.'

'Savings?'

'No.'

'Didn't she talk to you about her dream of having a restaurant one day?'

'Several times.'

'What did you reply?'

'Perhaps.'

'Did you intend to change your profession?'

'Not at that time.'

'You only made up your mind later, after two years of marriage, when she brought up the subject again and told you about a unique opportunity.'

He was flustered, but Maigret went on, relentless:

'You were jealous. Out of jealousy you made her stay at home instead of working as she wished to do. At that time, you lived in a two-room apartment on Rue de Turenne. Every evening you insisted she gave you an account of how she'd spent her day. Were you really convinced she loved you?'

'I believed so.'

'Without any ulterior motive?'

'There is none.'

'I believe your brother used to see you quite often?'

'He lived in Paris.'

'Did he go out with your wife?'

'Sometimes the three of us went out together.'

'The two of them never went out on their own?'

'Occasionally.'

'Your brother lived in lodgings in Rue Bréa, near Place des Ternes. Did your wife go and visit him in his room?'

Tormented, Meurant almost shouted:

'No!'

'Has she ever owned a pullover like the ones people wear to go skiing, a coarse, hand-knitted white wool pullover with a black-and-brown reindeer pattern? Did she ever go out in the winter wearing it with black trousers that tapered at the ankles?'

Frowning, he stared intently at Maigret.

'What are you driving at?'

'Answer.'

'Yes. Very rarely. I didn't like her going out into the street wearing trousers.'

'Have you often seen women dressed that way in the streets of Paris?'

'No.'

'Read this, Meurant.'

Maigret took out a document from a file, the statement of the landlady of the lodging house in Rue Bréa. She clearly remembered having Alfred Meurant as a tenant. He had occupied a room in her establishment on a monthly basis for a long time and still came back for a few days occasionally. He entertained a lot of women. She immediately recognized the photograph she was shown, which was that of Ginette Meurant. She even recalled having seen her in an unconventional get-up . . .

Then came the description of the pullover and trousers.

Had Ginette Meurant recently gone back to Rue Bréa?

The landlady's reply: less than a year ago, when Alfred Meurant was in Paris briefly.

'It's not true!' protested Meurant, pushing away the statement.

'Would you like to read the entire file? It contains at least thirty statements, all from hotel owners, including one in Saint-Cloud. Did your brother own a sky-blue convertible?'

Meurant's face provided the reply.

'He wasn't the only one. At the dance hall in Rue des Gravilliers, your wife was seen with some fifteen lovers.'

Maigret, heavy and solemn, filled a fresh pipe. He derived no pleasure from steering the conversation in this direction.

'It's not true!' moaned the husband again.

'She didn't ask to become your wife. She did nothing to encourage you. It took her three weeks to agree to go out with you, perhaps so as not to hurt you. She went with you to a hotel when you asked her to, because to her it meant nothing. You painted a picture of a rosy, comfortable existence, security, access to a bourgeois lifestyle. You more or less promised her that one day you'd fulfil her dream of a little restaurant.

'Out of jealousy, you wouldn't allow her to work.

'You didn't dance, and you barely liked the cinema.'

'We went every week.'

'The rest of the time, she was condemned to go there alone. In the evenings, you would read.'

'I've always dreamed of becoming more educated.'

'And she has always dreamed of something different. Are you beginning to understand?'

'I don't believe you.'

'However, you are certain that you have never told anyone else about the Chinese vase. And, on 27 February, you were not wearing your blue suit. You and your wife were the only people to have keys to the apartment on Boulevard de Charonne.'

The telephone rang. Maigret picked it up.

'Speaking, yes . . .'

Baron was on the other end of the line.

'She went out at around nine, at four minutes to nine to be precise, and headed towards Boulevard Voltaire.'

'Dressed how?'

'A floral dress and a brown wool coat. No hat.'

'And then?'

'She went into a shop selling travel goods and bought a cheap suitcase. She returned home with the suitcase. It must be warm inside because she opened the window. I can see her moving around and I imagine she's packing her bags.'

As he listened, Maigret watched Meurant, who suspected they were talking about his wife and looked worried.

'Nothing's happened to her?' he even asked at one point.

Maigret shook his head.

'Since there's a telephone in the concierge's lodge,'

Baron went on, 'I called a taxi which is parked a hundred metres away, in case she phones for one.'

'Very good. Keep me informed.'

And to Meurant:

'Just a moment . . .'

Maigret went into the inspectors' office and spoke to Janvier.

'You'd better take a service vehicle and get over to Boulevard de Charonne as fast as possible. It looks as if Ginette Meurant's about to do a runner. She may suspect that her husband has come here. She must be afraid of that.'

'How is he reacting?'

'I'd rather not be in his shoes.'

Maigret would also rather be dealing with something else.

'You're wanted on the phone, inspector.'

'Put the call through here.'

It was the public prosecutor, whose conscience wasn't entirely easy either.

'Hasn't anything happened?'

'They went home. They appear to have slept in separate rooms. Meurant went out early and is in my office right now.'

'What did you tell him? No doubt he refuses to believe you?'

'I'm in the inspectors' office. He's not yet sure whether to believe me. He's struggling. He's beginning to realize that he'll have to look the truth in the face.'

'You're not afraid that he'll . . .'

'There's every chance that she won't be there when he gets home. She's packing her bags.'

'And if he finds her?'

'After what I've had to put him through, she's not the one he'll be angry with.'

'He's not the sort to commit suicide?'

'Not before he's uncovered the truth.'

'Do you plan to expose it?'

Maigret said nothing but shrugged.

'As soon as there are any developments—'

'I'll telephone you or I'll drop into your office, sir.'

'Have you read the papers?'

'Only the headlines.'

Maigret hung up. Janvier had already left. It was better to keep Meurant there for a while, to prevent him from discovering his wife in the middle of packing her bags.

If he tracked her down later, it would be less risky. The most dangerous moment would be over. That was why Maigret, pipe in his mouth, paced up and down the long corridor, which was less suffocatingly warm, for a minute or two.

Then, glancing at his watch, he went into his office and found Meurant calmer and looking pensive.

'There's still a possibility you haven't mentioned,' objected Ginette's husband. 'One person at least must have known the secret of the Chinese vase.'

'The little girl's mother?'

'Yes: Juliette Perrin. She often used to visit Léontine Faverges and Cécile. Even if the old woman hadn't told

her anything about her money, the child might have
seen . . .'

'Do you think it didn't occur to me?'

'Why didn't you explore that avenue? Juliette Perrin
works in a nightclub. She mixes with all sorts of
people . . .'

He was clinging desperately to that hope, and Maigret
felt bad about disappointing him. But it was necessary.

'We investigated all her relations but got nowhere.

'Besides, there's one thing that neither Juliette Perrin
nor her casual or regular lovers could get hold of without
an accomplice.'

'What?'

'The blue suit. Do you know the child's mother?'

'No.'

'You never ran into her at Rue Manuel?'

'No. I knew that Cécile's mother was a nightclub hostess, but I have never had the occasion to meet her.'

'Don't forget that her daughter was murdered.'

For Meurant, another door was closing. He was still
seeking, groping, determined not to accept the truth.

'My wife could have mentioned it inadvertently.'

'To whom?'

'I don't know.'

'And also inadvertently handed over the key to your
apartment when she left for the cinema?'

Telephone. Janvier, this time, slightly out of breath.

'I'm calling from the concierge's, chief. The woman has
left in a taxi with the suitcase and a bulging brown bag.
I wrote down the registration number just in case. It

belongs to a firm in Levallois and will be easy to trace. Baron's following her in another taxi. Shall I wait here?'

'Yes.'

'Are you still with him?'

'Yes.'

'Presumably after he gets here I stay put?'

'That's best.'

'I'm going to park the car by one of the cemetery gates. It will be less obvious. Will you be letting him go soon?'

'Yes.'

Meurant was still trying to guess, and the effort brought the blood rushing to his head. He was utterly exhausted, utterly in despair too, but he managed to hold firm and even almost to smile.

'Is it my wife who's under surveillance?'

Maigret nodded.

'I suppose I'm going to be under surveillance too?'

Maigret made a vague gesture.

'I don't have a gun, believe me!'

'I know.'

'I don't intend to kill anyone, or to kill myself.'

'I know that too.'

'In any case, not now.'

He stood up and Maigret realized that he was close to breaking point, that the man was struggling not to burst into tears, sob and bang the walls with his clenched fists.

'Be strong, my friend.'

Meurant looked away, walked towards the door, not very steady on his feet. Maigret put his hand briefly on his shoulder.

'Come and see me whenever you like.'

Meurant finally left, without turning to face Maigret, without saying thank you, and the door closed behind him.

Baron was waiting outside the building, ready to carry on tailing him.

6.

At midday, as he was about to go home, Maigret received the first news of Ginette Meurant.

Dupeu telephoned from a bar in Rue Delambre close to Rue de la Gaité in the Montparnasse district. Dupeu was an excellent inspector who had only one fault: he reeled off his reports in a monotonous voice, as if he would never finish, piling on so many details that Maigret ended up only half listening.

'Get on with it!' he was tempted to say.

If anyone did interrupt him, Dupeu became so crest-fallen that they immediately regretted it.

'I'm in a bar called the Pickwick, chief, a hundred metres from Boulevard Montparnasse, and twelve minutes ago she arrived at the Hôtel de Concarneau opposite. It's a decent hotel that boasts hot and cold running water and a telephone in every room, a bathroom on each floor. She's in room 32 and it doesn't look as if she's in a hurry to leave because she argued over the price and rented the room for the week. Unless it's a trick.'

'Does she know she's been followed?'

'I'm certain she does. In the taxi, she turned around several times. On leaving Boulevard de Charonne, she showed the driver a visiting card which she took out of her handbag. When we reached Boulevard Saint-Michel, with me immediately behind her, she leaned over towards the driver. I could see her clearly through the rear window. He abruptly turned off to the right, into Faubourg Saint-Germain, then, for nearly ten minutes, he drove around in circles through the backstreets of Saint-Germain-des-Prés.

'I assume she was hoping to shake me off. When she realized it was impossible, she gave the driver further instructions and her taxi soon pulled up outside a building in Rue Monsieur-le-Prince.'

Maigret listened patiently, without interrupting.

'She asked the driver to wait and went inside. I followed her shortly afterwards and questioned the concierge. The person whom Ginette Meurant went to see was none other than Maître Lamblin, who lives on the first floor. She stayed there for some twenty minutes. When she came out, I had the impression she wasn't very pleased. Then she told the driver to bring her here. I assume you want me to keep her under surveillance?'

'Until someone comes to relieve you.'

Meanwhile, Janvier was probably still at Boulevard de Charonne, keeping an eye on the husband, backed up by Baron.

Was it solely to ask his advice that Ginette Meurant had visited the lawyer? Maigret doubted it. Before leaving his office, he gave instructions to Lucas, then headed for the bus stop.

Seven months earlier, on 27 February, the Meurants had barely any money, because they were unable to pay the draft due to be presented the next day. Furthermore, they owed the local shopkeepers money, as was their wont.

When a few days later the examining magistrate had asked Meurant to choose a lawyer, the picture-framer had objected that he couldn't afford to pay, and Pierre Duché had been appointed to represent him.

What had Ginette Meurant been living on since his arrest? As far as the police knew, from opening her letters, she hadn't received any postal orders. Nor did she appear to have cashed any cheques. Although she hadn't run up many expenses and had lived a reclusive existence in her apartment, she had still had to eat, and before the trial she'd bought the skirt and black coat she wore to court.

Was it possible that she had set aside some money, unbeknown to her husband, fiddling the housekeeping expenses as many women do?

Lamblin, at the Palais de Justice, had kept close to her. The lawyer was savvy enough to predict that the case would have sensational repercussions and that if he were then to represent the young woman, it would be a feather in his cap.

Maigret was perhaps mistaken, but he was convinced that Ginette Meurant had gone to Rue Monsieur-le-Prince to obtain money rather than to ask for an opinion.

Lamblin's reputation being what it was, he must have given her money, but in dribs and drabs. He had probably also advised her not to leave Paris but to lie low until further instructions.

Montparnasse had not been chosen by coincidence. Neither Meurant nor Ginette had lived in the neighbourhood, nor was it one of their haunts, so there was little chance that Meurant would go looking for his wife there.

Maigret was now back in the calm atmosphere of his home, having lunch with Madame Maigret. When he got back to his office, at two o'clock, a telephone message from Janvier informed him that Meurant had not left his apartment, where all was quiet.

He had to go and confer with the commissioner about an unpleasant case involving politics and it was four o'clock when Janvier called him again.

'Things are moving, chief. I don't know what's going to happen, but there's bound to be a development. He went out at two forty-five, carrying some bulky packages. Although they looked heavy, he didn't call a taxi. True, he didn't go far. A little later he went into a second-hand shop on Boulevard de Ménilmontant, and stayed there talking to the owner for a long time.'

'Did he see you?'

'Probably. It was hard to hide, because the area was almost deserted. He sold his watch, the gramophone, the records and a pile of books. Then he went home, came out again, this time with a huge bundle tied up in a bed sheet.

'He returned to the same shop, where he sold clothes, linen, cutlery and brass candlesticks.

'Now, he's back home, but I don't think he'll stay there for long.'

Janvier was right, and fifty minutes later, he called back.

'He went out once to go to Faubourg Saint-Antoine, to a picture-framer's. After a fairly long conversation, the two of them got into his van and drove to Rue de la Roquette, parking opposite Meurant's shop.

'They inspected the frames one by one. The man from Faubourg Saint-Antoine loaded a number of them into his van and gave Meurant some banknotes.

'I forgot to tell you that he's clean-shaven now. I don't know what he's doing in his workshop, but I've got the car just around the corner in case . . .'

At six o'clock in the evening, Maigret received the latest call from Janvier, who was phoning from Gare de Lyon.

'He's leaving in twelve minutes, chief. He bought a second-class ticket to Toulon. He's only carrying a small case. Right now, he's drinking a brandy at the bar; I can see him through the phone-booth window.'

'Is he looking at you?'

'Yes.'

'How does he seem?'

'He seems like a man hell-bent on one thing.'

'Make sure that he really does get on that train and then come back here.'

The train only stopped at Dijon, Lyon, Avignon and Marseille. Maigret telephoned the railway-station police in each of those towns, gave a description of the picture-framer and told them which carriage he was in. Then he called the Toulon Flying Squad.

The superintendent, whose name was Blanc, was around the same age as Maigret. They knew each other well because, before joining the Sûreté, Blanc had been at Quai des Orfèvres.

'Maigret here. I hope you're not too busy? I'm going to arrange for the prosecutor's office to send you a letter of request tomorrow, but it's best I put you in the picture right away. What time does the 6.17 p.m. train from Paris arrive in Toulon?'

'At 8.32 a.m.'

'Right. In carriage 10, unless he changes seats during the journey, you'll find a certain Meurant.'

'I've read the papers.'

'I'd like him tailed from the minute he gets off.'

'That's easy. Does he know the town?'

'I don't think he's ever been to the south, but I could be wrong. Meurant has a brother, Alfred.'

'I know him. I've had several dealings with him.'

'Is he in Toulon at present?'

'I'll be able to tell you in an hour or two. Would you like me to call you back?'

'At my home.'

He gave the number of Boulevard Richard-Lenoir.

'What do you know about Alfred Meurant's recent activities?'

'He generally lives in a guesthouse called Les Eucalyptus, outside the town, quite a way, actually, in the hills between Mont Faron and La Valette.'

'What kind of guesthouse?'

'The kind we keep an eye on. There are a number of them on the coast, between Marseille and Menton. The owner, Lisca, known as Freddo, was a barman for many years in Montmartre, Rue de Douai. Freddo married a pretty little minx, a former striptease artist, and they bought Les Eucalyptus.

'Freddo's the one who does the cooking, and people say he loves it. The place is set back from the road, at the end of a path that's a dead-end. In the summer, guests eat outdoors, under the trees.

'Highly respectable people from Toulon – doctors, officials, magistrates – go there for a meal from time to time.

'But the real clientele are the Riviera mafia who regularly go up to Paris.

'Girls too, in need of a change of scene.

'You see the type?'

'I see.'

'Two of the most loyal customers, almost year-round boarders, are Falconi and Scapucci.

'Both have long criminal records and are spotted from time to time around Pigalle.

'They're good friends of Alfred Meurant's. Openly, all three install slot machines in the region's bars. They also supply docile barmaids, whom they bring in from all around the country.

'They have several cars and often change them. For a while now, I've suspected them of handling cars stolen in Paris or the suburbs, falsifying the number plates and selling them off in Italy.

'I don't have any evidence yet. My men are on the case.'

'I have every reason to believe that Gaston Meurant is going to try to contact his brother.'

'If he goes to the right place, he'll have no trouble finding him, unless Alfred has given instructions for people to keep their mouths shut.'

'Should my Meurant buy a gun or try to obtain one, I'd like to be informed straight away.'

'Understood, Maigret. We'll do our best. What's the weather like up there?'

'Grey and cold.'

'Here it's beautifully sunny. By the way, I nearly forgot someone. Among Freddo's current clients, there's the man they call Kubik.'

Maigret had arrested him twelve years earlier following a raid on a jeweller's on Boulevard Saint-Martin.

'There's every chance that he was involved in the jewellery heist last month at Cours Albert-Premier, in Nice.'

Maigret knew that milieu well too, and he was slightly envious of Blanc. Like his colleagues, he preferred to deal with professionals because, with them, you knew at once what territory you were on and there were clear rules.

What was Gaston Meurant, alone in his compartment, going to do among those people?

Maigret had a long chat with Lucas, whom he put in charge of staking out Rue Delambre and choosing the inspectors who would take turns to keep watch.

Ginette Meurant had spent the afternoon in her hotel room, most likely sleeping. There was a telephone in every room as advertised outside, but all calls went through the operator.

According to the owner, who was from Auvergne, she had not made any calls and he was certain that the hotel had not requested any calls to be put through to the south of France. All the same, an expert was busy connecting the line to a wiretap.

Ginette had held firm for a long time. Either she was exceptionally wily or, since the murders in Rue Manuel, she had not tried even once to contact the man she had accompanied to Rue Victor-Massé for months, up until 26 February.

It was as if, suddenly, from one day to the next, that man had ceased to exist. And he did not appear to have tried to contact her either.

The police had thought of the possibility of prearranged signals. They had watched the windows of the apartment on Boulevard de Charonne, studied the position of the curtains, which could be significant, the lights, and the comings and goings across the street.

Nor had the man shown up at the court, or in the vicinity of the Palais de Justice.

It was so exceptional that Maigret was filled with admiration.

Now she finally came out, in search of a cheap restaurant in this unfamiliar neighbourhood. She ate alone at a table, reading a magazine. Then she went and bought some more on the corner of Boulevard Montparnasse, together with a few trashy novels, and returned to her room where the light stayed on until after midnight.

Meanwhile, Gaston Meurant was still in the train. At Dijon, then Lyon, an inspector walked through the corridors, checked that he hadn't moved from his corner, and the intelligence reached Boulevard Richard-Lenoir where Maigret reached out in the dark to pick up the telephone.

Another day dawned. After Montélimar, Meurant encountered the atmosphere of Provence and it would probably not be long before, his face pressed to the window, he would be watching a landscape that was new to him flash past in the sunlight.

Marseille . . . Maigret was shaving when he received the call from Gare Saint-Charles.

Meurant was still in the train as it continued on its way. He hadn't bluffed: he was indeed going to Toulon.

In Paris, the weather continued to be grey and the faces in the bus were glum or scowling. On the desk, a pile of administrative documents awaited him.

An inspector – Maigret couldn't remember which one – telephoned from the bar in Rue Delambre.

'She's asleep. In any case, the curtains are drawn and she hasn't asked for her breakfast.'

The train pulled into Toulon. Gaston Meurant, clutching his little case, wandered around the square, disoriented, a police officer on his heels. Eventually he walked into the Hôtel des Voyageurs, where he chose the cheapest room.

A little later, it became clear that he didn't know the town because he immediately lost his way walking through the streets and had difficulty finding Boulevard de Strasbourg where he went into a big brasserie. He ordered, not a brandy but a coffee, and questioned at length the waiter, who seemed unable to provide him with the information he required.

By midday, he hadn't found what he was looking for and, comically, it was Superintendent Blanc who was growing impatient.

'I wanted to see your fellow for myself,' he said to Maigret over the phone. 'I found him in a bar on Quai Cronstadt. He can't have slept much on the train. He looks like a poor, exhausted wretch who's pursuing an obsession. He's going about it the wrong way. So far, he's been into around fifteen cafés and bars. Each time, he orders a mineral water. People assume he's a beggar and give him dirty looks. His question is always the same:

'"Do you know Alfred Meurant?"

'Barmen and waiters are wary, especially of course those who do know him. They reply with a vague shrug. Others ask:

'"What's he done?"

'"I don't know. He lives in Toulon."

'The inspector who's on his tail is beginning to feel sorry for him and is almost tempted to tip him off.

'At the rate Meurant's going, this could carry on for ages and he's going to end up broke from buying all that mineral water.'

Maigret was familiar enough with Toulon to know at least three places where Meurant could have got news of his brother. The picture-framer would reach the right area in the end. If he went further into the backstreets around Quai Cronstadt, or if fate took him to the Mourillon district, he would eventually find the information he was so doggedly seeking.

In Rue Delambre, Ginette Meurant had opened her curtains, ordered coffee and croissants and gone back to bed to read.

She did not telephone Maître Lamblin, or anyone else. Nor did she try to find out what had become of her husband or whether the police were still following her.

Wouldn't she eventually crack?

The lawyer, meanwhile, was taking no steps and was going about his usual business.

An idea occurred to Maigret, who went into the inspectors' office and walked over to Lucas.

'What time did she go and see her lawyer yesterday?'

'Around eleven, if my memory's correct. I can check the report.'

'No need. In any case, there was still time to place an ad in the evening papers. Get hold of yesterday's papers, and this morning's, and later, this evening's. Go through the classified ads.'

Lamblin was known to be a man of few scruples. If Ginette Meurant were to ask him to place an ad, would he have any qualms? It was unlikely.

If Maigret's hunch was right, it would suggest that she didn't know her former lover's whereabouts.

If on the other hand she did, and if he hadn't moved since March, could Lamblin have made a telephone call for her? Could she not have made it herself during the twenty minutes she had spent at the lawyer's?

One detail had struck Maigret from the start of the investigation in the spring. The liaison between the young woman and the man described by Nicolas Cajou had lasted for many months. Throughout the winter they'd met several times a week, which seemed to suggest that the lover lived in Paris.

But all the same, they met in a lodging house.

Did that mean that, for one reason or another, the man could not entertain his mistress at home?

Was he married? Did he not live alone?

Maigret had not discovered the answer.

'Just in case,' he said to Lucas, 'try to find out whether there was a phone call to Toulon yesterday from Lamblin's number.'

There was nothing else he could do but wait. In Toulon, Gaston Meurant was still looking for his brother, and it was half past four when, in a little café where men were playing boules outside, he finally obtained the information he wanted.

The waiter pointed out the hill to him and launched into a complicated explanation.

By that time Maigret already knew that the brother, Alfred, was in Toulon and that he hadn't left Les Eucalyptus for over a week.

He gave instructions to Superintendent Blanc.

'Do you have a youngster among your men who isn't known to those people?'

'My men don't remain anonymous for long, but I have one who arrived three days ago from Brest. His job is chiefly to look after the dockyard and he certainly won't have been noticed yet.'

'Send him to Les Eucalyptus.'

'Understood. He'll be there before Meurant, because the poor boy has set out on foot, either to save money or because he has no idea of the distance. And most likely he'll lose his way a few times on the paths in the hills . . .'

It pained Maigret not to be on the spot. Despite their speed and precision, the reports he received were still second-hand intelligence.

Two or three times that day he was tempted to go to

Rue Delambre and renew contact with Ginette Meurant. He had the impression, for no particular reason, that he was beginning to know her a little better. Perhaps, now, he would be able to ask the specific questions that she would end up answering?

It was still too soon. If Meurant had gone straight to Toulon, he must have his reasons.

During the investigation, the police had got nothing out of the brother, but that didn't mean there was nothing to be got out of him.

Gaston Meurant was unarmed, that was now a fact, and as for the rest, the only thing to do was to wait.

Maigret went home in a grumpy mood. Madame Maigret refrained from questioning him and he ate dinner in his slippers, became engrossed in reading the newspapers, then turned on the wireless, looked for a station that wasn't too chatty and, unable to find one, switched it off with a sigh of relief.

At ten o'clock, he had a call from Toulon. It wasn't Blanc, who was attending a dinner, but the young inspector from Brest, a certain Le Goënec, whom the Flying Squad superintendent had sent to Les Eucalyptus.

'I'm calling you from the railway station.'

'Where's Gaston Meurant?'

'In the waiting room. He's taking the night train in an hour and a half. He paid his hotel bill.'

'Did he go to Les Eucalyptus?'

'Yes.'

'Did he see his brother?'

'Yes. When he arrived, at around six, three men and the

landlady were playing cards in the bar. There was Kubik, Falconi and Alfred Meurant, all three relaxed. I got there before him and asked if I could have dinner and a room for the night. The owner came out of his kitchen to size me up and eventually said yes. I was carrying a haversack and said I was hitching around the Riviera looking for a job.'

'Did they believe you?'

'I don't know. While waiting for dinner time, I sat in a corner, ordered some white wine, and read. They glanced in my direction every now and then, but they didn't seem too suspicious. Gaston Meurant turned up fifteen minutes after me. It was already dark. The glass garden door opened and he stood there on the threshold, looking around goggle-eyed.'

'How did the brother react?'

'He stared hard at the newcomer, stood up, flung his cards on to the table and went over to him.

'"What are you doing here? Who squealed?"'

'The others pretended not to be listening.

'"I need to talk to you," said Gaston Meurant, adding hurriedly: "Don't be scared. It's not you I'm angry with."'

'"Come!" ordered his brother, heading upstairs to the bedrooms.

'I couldn't follow them straight away. The others stopped talking, worried, and began to look at me differently. They were probably beginning to make a connection between my arrival and Meurant's.

'So I just carried on drinking my wine and reading.

'Although the dump's freshly painted, it's fairly old and shoddily built, and you can hear every sound.

'The two brothers locked themselves in a room on the first floor and initially Alfred Meurant's voice was loud and tough. Although you couldn't hear the words, it was clear he was angry.

'Then the other one, the Parisian, began to speak, in a much more muffled voice. He went on for a long time, virtually without stopping, as if he were telling a story he'd rehearsed.

'The landlady winked at her companions and came to set my place, as if to create a distraction. Then the others ordered aperitifs. Kubik went to talk to Freddo in the kitchen and I didn't see him again.

'I suspect he made a run for it as a precaution, because I heard a car engine.'

'You have no idea what happened upstairs?'

'Only that they stayed locked inside the room for an hour and a half. In the end, it sounded as if Gaston Meurant, the Parisian, had the upper hand, and it was his brother who spoke in a quiet voice.

'I'd finished eating by the time they came down. Alfred Meurant looked miserable, as if things hadn't gone the way he'd wanted, while the other man, on the contrary, looked more relaxed than when he'd arrived.

'"You'll have a drink, won't you?" suggested Alfred.

'"No, thank you."

'"Are you leaving already?"

'"Yes."

'They both looked at me and frowned.

'"I'll drive you back into town."

'"There's no need."

'"Don't you want me to call you a taxi?"

'"No, thank you."

'They spoke grudgingly, and you could tell that the words were only to fill the silence.

'Gaston Meurant went out. His brother closed the door behind him, was on the verge of saying something to the landlady and Falconi, but then changed his mind on spotting me.

'I wasn't sure what to do. I didn't dare telephone the chief to ask for instructions. I thought it best to follow Gaston Meurant. I went outside as if going out for a breath of fresh air after dinner, without taking my haversack.

'I found my man walking at a steady pace down the road back into town.

'He stopped for a bite to eat on Boulevard de la République, and then he went to the station to ask about train times. Next, he went back to the Hôtel des Voyageurs, picked up his case and paid his bill.

'Since then, he's been waiting. He's not reading the newspapers, he's doing nothing, just looking straight ahead, his eyes half-closed. You couldn't say he was smiling, but he does seem quite pleased with himself.'

'Wait till he gets on the train and call me back to let me know which carriage he's in.'

'OK. Tomorrow morning I'll make my report to the superintendent.'

Inspector Le Goënec was about to hang up when Maigret had second thoughts.

'I'd like to make certain that Alfred Meurant doesn't leave Les Eucalyptus.'

'Do you want me to go back there? Don't you think my cover's blown?'

'I just need one of your men to keep an eye on the place. I'd also like the telephone to be tapped. If anyone calls Paris, or any other city, I want to be informed as soon as possible.'

The routine began again, in the reverse direction: Marseille, Avignon, Lyon and Dijon were alerted. They were allowing Gaston Meurant to travel alone, like a big boy, but were passing him from hand to hand, as it were.

He wasn't due to arrive in Paris until eleven thirty.

Maigret went to bed, and felt as if he'd barely slept when his wife woke him, bringing him his first cup of coffee. The sky was clear at last and he could see the sun above the rooftops opposite. People in the street walked with a lighter step.

'Will you be home for lunch?'

'I doubt it. I'll phone you before midday.'

Ginette Meurant hadn't left the hotel in Rue Delambre. She was still spending most of her time in bed, only going downstairs to eat and to renew her stash of magazines and romantic novels.

'No news, Maigret?' inquired the public prosecutor.

'Nothing specific yet, but I shouldn't be surprised if there were some developments very soon.'

'What's become of Meurant?'

'He's on the train.'

'Which train?'

'The one from Toulon. He's on his way back. He went to see his brother.'

'What happened between them?'

'They had a long conversation, at first stormy, apparently, and then calmer. The brother isn't happy. Gaston Meurant, however, is acting like a man who knows where he's going at last.'

What else could Maigret say? He had nothing precise to tell the prosecutor. For two days he'd been groping around in a sort of fog, but even so, like Gaston Meurant, he had the feeling that something was becoming clearer.

He was tempted to go to the station a little later and wait for the picture-framer himself. But wouldn't it be better for him to stay at the centre of operations? And, if he followed Gaston Meurant in the street, might he not ruin everything?

He chose Lapointe, knowing that would please him, and then another inspector, Neveu, who hadn't been involved in the case so far. For ten years, Neveu had worked in the traffic division and had specialized in pickpockets.

Lapointe left for the station unaware that Neveu would shortly be following him.

But first of all, Maigret had to give him precise instructions.

7.

With his pale complexion, ginger hair, blue eyes and mild manner, Gaston Meurant had probably always been shy, but above all he was patient and determined and had worked hard to carve out his own happy little world among Paris' three million inhabitants.

He had learned his craft to the best of his ability, a delicate craft that demanded discernment and attention to detail, and it is not hard to imagine the satisfaction he must have felt on overcoming the biggest hurdle, the day he had set up his own business, even though it was at the far end of a courtyard.

Was it his shyness, or his caution, the fear of making a mistake, that had made him avoid women for a long time? When being questioned, he had admitted to Maigret that, until meeting Ginette, he had contented himself with little – the minimum – brief brushes with women, which he considered shameful, except for a relationship he'd had at around eighteen with a woman who was much older than him, and which had lasted only a few weeks.

The day when, blushing, he had finally asked a woman to marry him, he was well over thirty and fate had it that she was a girl who, a few months later, told him that she was unable to have children, whereas he'd been waiting impatiently for her to announce a forthcoming birth.

He had not been outraged. He accepted it, just as he accepted that she was so different from the companion of his dreams.

They were a couple, despite everything. He wasn't alone, even if there wasn't always a light in the window when he came home in the evening and he was often the one who cooked dinner, and afterwards they had nothing to say to each other.

Her dream had been to live amid the hustle and bustle of her own restaurant, and he had given in, with no illusions, fully aware that the venture could only end in failure.

Then, without showing any bitterness, he had returned to his workshop and his frames, obliged, from time to time, to go and ask his aunt for help.

During those years of marital life, as during the preceding years, he gave no sign of anger or impatience. He followed his path with a quiet doggedness, bowing his large ginger head when necessary, raising it when fate seemed to be smiling on him.

In short, he had built a little world of his own around his love and he clung to it with everything he had.

Did that not explain the hatred that had suddenly hardened in his eyes when Maigret had testified in court, painting a very different picture of Ginette from the one he had created?

Acquitted against his will, so to speak, released because of the suspicion that now hung over his wife, he had still left the Palais de Justice with her, side by side; and although not arm in arm, they had gone back to their home on Boulevard de Charonne.

But he had not slept in their bed. Twice, three times, she had come to talk to him, trying perhaps to tempt him, but she'd ended up sleeping alone, while he'd spent most of the night awake in the dining room.

At that point, however, he was still fighting, resolutely doubting. Perhaps he would have been capable of believing again. But for how long? Could life have continued as before? Would it not have gone through a series of painful ups and downs before finally falling apart?

Alone and unshaven, he had stood gazing at a hotel façade. To give himself courage, he had drunk three brandies. And then he had faltered before walking through the daunting entrance to Quai des Orfèvres.

Had Maigret been wrong to talk to him so heartlessly, pushing the button that would have been pushed sooner or later?

Maigret could not have acted differently, even had he wanted to. Meurant acquitted, Meurant not guilty meant that there was a man at large who had slit Léontine Faverges' throat and then suffocated a little four-year-old girl, a devious, cold-blooded killer who had framed another man and had almost succeeded in seeing him convicted.

Maigret had acted in the heat of the moment, suddenly forcing Meurant to open his eyes, to finally face the truth, and it was a different man who had left his office, a man for whom nothing mattered more than his mission.

He had ploughed on, feeling neither hunger nor tiredness, going from one train to another, unable to stop before arriving at his goal.

Did he suspect that Maigret had set up a surveillance network around him, that the police were waiting for him as he passed through the stations and that there was someone constantly tailing him, ready to intervene at the last minute if necessary?

He didn't appear to be worried about it, convinced that police cunning could not thwart his determination.

There were telephone calls after telephone calls, reports after reports. Lucas had combed through the classified ads in vain. The tapping of Ginette Meurant's hotel telephone in Rue Delambre had yielded nothing.

The lawyer Lamblin had not put a call through to the south, or to any other city.

In Toulon Alfred Meurant, the brother, had not moved from Les Eucalyptus, nor had he made any telephone calls either.

They were faced with a void, a void in which there was only a solitary, silent man behaving as if in a dream.

At eleven forty Lapointe called from Gare de Lyon.

'He's just arrived, chief. He's eating a sandwich in the buffet. He's still got his little case. Was it you who sent Neveu to the station?'

'Yes. Why?'

'I was wondering if you wanted him to relieve me. Neveu's in the buffet too, right next to Meurant.'

'Don't worry about him. Carry on.'

A quarter of an hour later, it was Inspector Neveu's turn to report back.

'I've done it, chief. I bumped into him on the way out. He didn't notice anything. He's got a gun. A large automatic, probably a Smith and Wesson, in the right pocket of his jacket. It's not too visible under his raincoat.'

'Has he left the station?'

'Yes. He got on to a bus and I saw Lapointe jump on behind him.'

'You can come back.'

Meurant had not visited a gunsmith's. He must have got his hands on the automatic in Toulon, and it could only have been given to him by his brother.

What exactly had happened between the two men, on the first floor of the bizarre family guesthouse which was a gangsters' favourite haunt?

Gaston Meurant knew now that his brother had also had intimate relations with Ginette, and yet that wasn't the reason he'd gone to confront him.

In making the trip to Toulon, had he not been hoping to find out about the short man with very dark hair who, several times a week, had accompanied his wife to Rue Victor-Massé?

Did he have a reason to believe that his brother knew something? And had he finally discovered what he was looking for – a name, a vital clue that the police had been seeking for several months in vain?

It was possible. It was likely, because he had demanded that his brother give him a gun.

If Alfred Meurant had talked, it wasn't out of affection for his brother, in any case. Was he afraid? Had Gaston threatened him? With some revelation? Or of doing him in one day?

Maigret asked to be put through to Toulon, and

managed, not without difficulty, to get hold of Detective Chief Inspector Blanc.

'It's me again, old friend. I apologize for all the work I'm giving you. We may need Alfred Meurant any minute. We won't necessarily be able to locate him when we need him, because I wouldn't be surprised if he had a sudden urge to go on a trip. So far, I've got nothing on him. Could you arrest him on some plausible enough pretext and keep him for a few hours?'

'Certainly. That's not difficult. I always have questions to ask that bunch.'

'Thank you. Try to find out whether he owned a fairly high-calibre automatic and whether it's still in his room.'

'Understood. Nothing new?'

'Not yet.'

Maigret almost added that it wouldn't be long. He had just told his wife not to expect him home for lunch and, loath to leave his office, had ordered sandwiches from the Brasserie Dauphine.

He was still sorry he wasn't out there following Gaston Meurant himself. He smoked pipe after pipe, impatient, constantly glancing at the telephone. The sun was shining and the autumnal leaves on the trees gave the Seine riverbanks a festive look.

'Is that you, chief? I've got to be quick. I'm at Gare de l'Est. He's put his case in left-luggage and has just bought a ticket to Chelles.'

'In Seine-et-Marne?'

'Yes. The slow train leaves in a few minutes. I'd better go. I presume you want me to stay on his tail?'

'Of course!'

'No specific instructions?'

What was in the back of Lapointe's mind? Had he suspected the reason for Neveu's presence at Gare de Lyon?

Maigret grunted:

'Nothing particular. Do as you think best.'

He knew Chelles, some twenty kilometres from Paris, between the canal and the Marne. He remembered a huge caustic soda factory in front of which barges were always being loaded and where once, when he was passing through the area on a Sunday morning, he had seen an entire flotilla of canoes.

The temperature had risen over the past twenty-four hours, but the maintenance man in charge of the Police Judiciaire heating system hadn't regulated the boiler and the heat in Maigret's office was suffocating.

He ate a sandwich standing at the window, vaguely staring out at the Seine. He took the occasional sip of beer and kept glancing restlessly at the telephone.

The train, which stopped at every station, would take at least half an hour, perhaps an hour, to reach Chelles.

The inspector keeping watch on Rue Delambre was the first to call.

'No change, chief. She's just come out and she's having lunch in the same restaurant, at the same table, as if she were already a regular.'

As far as they could tell, she was still strong-willed enough not to make contact with her lover.

Was he the person who, back in February, before the

double murder of Rue Manuel, had given her instructions as to what to do afterwards? Was she afraid of him?

Which of them had had the idea of the telephone call that had led to Gaston Meurant being charged?

At first, Meurant had not come under suspicion. He had gone to the police spontaneously and presented himself as the nephew of Léontine Faverges, whose death he had learned about from the newspapers.

There had been no reason to search his home.

But someone had grown impatient. Someone was in a hurry to see the investigation take a particular direction.

Three or four days had passed before the anonymous telephone call came, revealing that there was a certain blue suit with bloodstains on it hanging in a wardrobe at Boulevard de Charonne.

Lapointe still gave no sign of life. Now it was Toulon calling.

'He's in my inspectors' office. They're asking him a few trivial questions and we'll keep him until we hear back from you. We'll find some pretext or other. We've searched his room but found no gun. However, my men state that he was in the habit of carrying an automatic, which he's been sent down for twice.'

'Has he had other convictions?'

'Never anything major, other than on charges of procuring. He's too shrewd.'

'Thank you. I'll speak to you later. I'm hanging up because I'm expecting an important call any moment now.'

He went into the adjacent office where Janvier had just arrived.

'You'd better be ready to leave and make sure there's a free car in the yard.'

He began to regret not having told Lapointe the entire story. He recalled a film about Malaya in which an indigenous character enters in a frenzied state, suddenly possessed by a diabolical fury. Wielding a dagger, he walks straight ahead, his pupils dilated, killing everything that crosses his path.

Gaston Meurant was neither Malay nor in a frenzied state. Even so, for more than twenty-four hours now, had he not been on a mission, and was he not capable of dispatching anything that got in his way?

The telephone, at last. Maigret leaped towards the desk.

'Is that you, Lapointe?'

'Yes, chief.'

'In Chelles?'

'Further. I'm not exactly sure where I am. Between the canal and the Marne, around two kilometres from Chelles. I'm not certain because we took a roundabout route.'

'Did Meurant appear to know the way?'

'He didn't ask anyone. He must have been given precise directions. He stopped every so often to identify a crossroads and eventually took a dirt track that leads down to the river. At the intersection of this path and the old towpath, which is now just a footpath, there's an inn, where I'm calling you from. The landlady warned me that out of season she doesn't serve food and doesn't rent out rooms. Her husband is the ferryman. Meurant walked past the place without stopping.

'Two hundred metres upriver, there's a tumbledown shack with geese and ducks wandering around freely.'

'Is that where Meurant went?'

'He didn't go in. He spoke to an old lady who pointed to the river.'

'Where is he now?'

'Standing on the riverbank, leaning up against a tree. The old woman is over eighty. People call her Mother Goose. The innkeeper says she's half mad. Her name's Joséphine Millard. Her husband died years ago. Since then, she's always worn the same black dress and it's rumoured that she never takes it off, not even to go to bed. When she needs something, she makes her way to the Saturday market and sells a goose or a duck.'

'Did she have any children?'

'It's so long ago that the woman from the inn can't remember. As she says, it was before her time.'

'Is that all?'

'No. There's a man living at her place.'

'Permanently?'

'For the past few months, yes. Before, he used to disappear for a few days at a time.'

'What does he do?'

'Nothing. He chops wood. He reads. He fishes. He patched up an old rowing-boat. Right now, he's out fishing. I saw him from a distance in the boat, which he had moored to some poles on a bend in the river.'

'What does he look like?'

'I couldn't tell. The innkeeper describes him as dark-haired and thickset, with a hairy chest.'

'Short?'

'Yes.'

There was a silence. Then tentatively, as if embarrassed, Lapointe asked:

'Are you coming, chief?'

Lapointe wasn't afraid, but he must have sensed that he was going to have to take on responsibilities beyond his capability.

'It will take you less than half an hour to drive here.'

'I'm on my way.'

'What do I do in the meantime?'

Maigret hesitated, and finally said:

'Nothing.'

'Shall I stay put here at the inn?'

'Can you see Meurant from where you are?'

'Yes.'

'In that case, don't move.'

Maigret walked into the next-door office and beckoned to Janvier, who was waiting. As he was about to leave, he changed his mind and went over to Lucas.

'Go up to Records and see if there's anything under the name of Millard.'

'Yes, chief. Should I phone you somewhere?'

'No. I don't know where I'll be exactly. Beyond Chelles, somewhere by the Marne. If you need to get in touch with me urgently, ask the local gendarmerie for the name of an inn about two kilometres upriver.'

Janvier took the wheel of the little black car, because Maigret had never wanted to learn to drive.

'Any news, chief?'

'Yes.'

Janvier didn't dare press him and, after a long silence, Maigret muttered in a frustrated tone:

'Only I don't know what exactly.'

He was in no great hurry to get there. He preferred not to admit it, even to himself.

'Do you know the way?'

'I've occasionally been there for Sunday lunch with my wife and children.'

They drove through the outskirts, reached the first wasteland areas and then the first fields. In Chelles, they stopped at a crossroads, unsure of the way.

'If it's upriver, we should turn right.'

'Try.'

As they left the town, a car from the gendarmerie overtook them, siren blaring, and Janvier glanced at Maigret in silence.

Maigret was quiet too. Much further on, he said, chewing on his pipe:

'I presume it's over now.'

Because the gendarmerie car was heading for the Marne, which was now visible between the trees. To the right was an inn with yellow-painted bricks. A woman was standing on the doorstep, looking agitated.

The gendarmerie vehicle, which couldn't go any further, had stopped by the path. Maigret and Janvier got out of their car. The woman was gesticulating and shouting something at them which they couldn't hear.

They walked towards the shack surrounded by geese and ducks. The gendarmes, who had reached it first, called out to two men who appeared to be waiting for them. One was Lapointe. From a distance, the other looked like Gaston Meurant.

There were three gendarmes, including a lieutenant. An old woman in the doorway was gazing at all these people and shaking her head, as if unable to understand what was happening. Nobody, in fact, understood, except perhaps Meurant and Lapointe.

Mechanically, Maigret looked around for a body but couldn't see one. Lapointe said:

'In the water . . .'

But there was nothing to be seen in the water either.

As for Gaston Meurant, he was calm, almost smiling, and when Maigret finally made up his mind to look him in the eye, the picture-framer appeared to be silently thanking him.

Lapointe explained, as much for his chief's benefit as for the gendarmes:

'The man stopped fishing and untied his boat from the poles you see over there.'

'Who is he?'

'I don't know his name. He was wearing coarse linen trousers and a sailor's roll-neck pullover. He began to row across the river against the current.'

'Where were you?' asked the lieutenant.

'At the inn. I was watching from the window. I'd just telephoned Detective Chief Inspector Maigret . . .'

He indicated his boss and the officer, embarrassed, walked towards him.

'I apologize, inspector. You were the last person I

expected to meet here so I didn't recognize you. Your man had the innkeeper call us, but she simply said that a man had just been killed and had fallen into the water. I informed the Flying Squad immediately.'

The sound of an engine could be heard from the direction of the inn.

'Here they are!'

The newcomers added to the chaos and confusion. This was the Seine-et-Marne département, which was outside Maigret's jurisdiction.

But they all turned towards him.

'Shouldn't we handcuff him?'

'That's up to you, lieutenant. Personally, I don't think it's necessary.'

Meurant was no longer febrile. He listened distractedly to what was being said, as if it did not concern him. Most of the time, he stared downriver into the murky waters of the Marne.

Lapointe continued:

'While he rowed, the man in the boat had his back to the riverbank. So he couldn't see Meurant, who was standing by this tree.'

'Did you know he was going to shoot?'

'I was unaware that he had a gun.'

Maigret's face remained inscrutable. But Janvier glanced at him as if he had suddenly realized what was happening.

'As the bow touched the shore, the rower stood up and grabbed the anchor, then, just as he turned around, he found himself face to face with Meurant, who was barely three metres away.

'I don't know if any words were exchanged. I was too far away.

'Almost immediately, Meurant pulled an automatic out of his pocket and extended his right arm.

'The other man, standing in the boat, must have been hit by two bullets shot in quick succession. He dropped the anchor. His arms flailed, and he fell into the water face first . . .'

Now they all gazed at the river. The rain of the past few days had made the yellowish waters swell and form strong eddies in places.

'I asked the woman from the inn to call the gendarmerie and I ran—'

'Do you have a gun?'

'No.'

Lapointe added, perhaps rashly:

'There was no danger.'

The gendarmes were baffled. So were the men from the Flying Squad. Even though they had read the report of the trial in the newspapers, they didn't know the details of the case.

'Meurant didn't try to run away. He stayed put, watching the body vanish then reappear two or three times, each time a little further away, before sinking once and for all.

'When I reached him, he dropped his gun. I didn't touch it.'

The automatic was embedded in the mud on the path, next to a dead branch.

'Did he say anything?'

'Only two words:

'"It's over."'

And indeed, Gaston Meurant's struggle was over. His body seemed limper, his face puffy with exhaustion.

He was not jubilant, felt no wish to explain or justify himself. It was his business and his alone.

He believed he had done what he had to do.

Would he have found peace in any other way? Would he find it now?

The Melun public prosecutor was on his way to the scene. The madwoman in her doorway was still shaking her head, never having seen so many people around her house.

'It is possible,' Maigret told his colleagues, 'that when you search the shack, you'll make some interesting discoveries.'

He could have stayed with them and watched the search.

'Gentlemen, I'll send you all the intelligence you'll need.'

He would not be taking Meurant to Paris, because Meurant no longer belonged to Quai des Orfèvres, or to the Seine public prosecutor.

It was in Melun that he would appear before the court for the second time.

Maigret turned to Lapointe and Janvier:

'Are you coming, boys?'

He shook hands with those around him. Then, as he turned to leave, he darted a final glance at Ginette's husband.

Suddenly aware of his exhaustion no doubt, Meurant was leaning against a tree, watching Maigret leave with a sort of sadness.

8.

Few words were spoken during the return drive. Several times, Lapointe opened his mouth, but Maigret's silence was so dense, so resolute, that he didn't dare say anything.

Janvier was at the wheel, and he gradually had the feeling that he understood.

A few kilometres' difference and they were the ones who would have been bringing Gaston Meurant back.

'Maybe it's for the best,' muttered Janvier as if talking to himself.

Maigret neither agreed nor disagreed. What exactly had Janvier been referring to?

The three of them walked up the stairs of the Police Judiciaire, and parted in the corridor, Lapointe and Janvier to go into the inspectors' office, and Maigret to enter his, where he hung his coat and hat in the cupboard.

He didn't touch the bottle of brandy which he kept in reserve for certain customers. He barely had the time to fill a pipe before Lucas knocked and placed a bulky file in front of him.

'I found this upstairs, chief. It looks as if it all stacks up.'

And it did stack up. It was the file of Pierre Millard, known as Pierrot, thirty-two years old, born in Paris in the Goutte-d'Or district.

He'd had a criminal record from the age of eighteen,

when he'd appeared in front of the Seine tribunal for pro-curement. Then came two further convictions for the same offence, with a stint in Fresnes prison, then a convic-tion for causing grievous bodily harm in Marseille and finally five years at Fontevrault jail for the burglary of a factory in Bordeaux and inflicting grievous bodily harm on a night watchman who had been found half-dead.

He had been freed eighteen months ago. Since then, the police had lost track of him.

Maigret picked up the telephone and called Toulon.

'Is that you, Blanc? Well, my friend, it's all over. Two bullets in the body of a certain Pierre Millard, known as Pierrot.'

'A short, swarthy fellow?'

'Yes. They're looking for his body in the Marne, where he fell head first. Does the name mean anything to you?'

'I'll have to ask my men. I think he was prowling around here just over a year ago.'

'It's likely. He was released from Fontevrault and banned from residence in Paris. Perhaps, now that you know his name, you could ask Alfred Meurant a few precise ques-tions? Is he still with you?'

'Yes. Shall I call you back?'

'Thank you.'

In Paris, in any case, Millard had been cautious. Although he went into the city often, almost every day, he was care-ful not to sleep there. He had found a safe place to stay on the banks of the Marne, in the shack belonging to the old woman, who must have been his grandmother.

He had lain low since the double murder in Rue Manuel.

Ginette Meurant hadn't tried to join him. She had sent no message. Perhaps she didn't know where he was hiding.

If things had gone differently, especially if Nicolas Cajou had not testified, would Gaston Meurant have been wrongly sentenced to death or to forced labour for life? At best, given there was a slight doubt and in the light of his honourable past, he would have got away with twenty years.

Millard, then, once the verdict was given, could have come out of his hiding place, made his way to the country-side or abroad, where all Ginette had to do was join him.

'Hello, yes . . .'

The call was from Seine-et-Marne. It was the Gournay Flying Squad informing him that they had discovered gold coins, bearer bonds and a quantity of banknotes in an old wallet.

All in a metal box buried in the poultry pen.

They hadn't yet retrieved the body but hoped to find it at the Chelles weir, where the lock-keeper was used to fishing out most of those who drowned in the millstream.

They had made other discoveries in the old woman's house, including an ancient trunk in the attic containing a nineteenth-century bridal gown, a suit, other dresses, some of puce or pale-blue silk, trimmed with yellowed lace. The most startling find was a Zouave uniform from the turn of the century.

Mother Goose barely remembered her family, and seemed unaffected by the death of her grandson. When the police talked of taking her to Gournay to question her,

her only worry was her birds and they had to promise they would bring her back that evening.

They would probably not ask her about her past, or her children, all trace of whom had been lost.

It was likely she would live for many more years in her riverside shack.

'Janvier!'

'Yes, chief.'

'Can you take Lapointe with you and go to Rue Delambre?'

'Should I bring her in?'

'Yes.'

'Don't you think I should get a warrant?'

As an officer of the Police Judiciaire, Maigret was authorized to sign an arrest warrant, which he did on the spot.

'What if she asks any questions?'

'Say nothing.'

'Should I handcuff her?'

'Only if it's necessary.'

Blanc called back from Toulon.

'I have just asked him some interesting questions.'

'Did you tell him that Millard was dead?'

'Of course.'

'Did he seem surprised?'

'No. He didn't even bother to pretend.'

'Did he spill the beans?'

'More or less. It's up to you to judge. He was careful not to say anything that might incriminate himself. He admits to knowing Millard. He met him several times, more than seven years ago, in Paris and Marseille. Then Millard got five years and Alfred Meurant heard no more from him.

'On his release from Fontevrault, Millard came back and hung around Marseille, then Toulon. He was in quite a bad way and was trying to get back in the saddle. His plan, from what Meurant says, was to stop tinkering and to pull off a big job that would set him up once and for all.

'As soon as he'd refurbished his wardrobe, he planned to go to Paris.

'He only stayed on the Riviera for a few weeks. Meurant admits he gave him small sums of money, introduced him to friends, who also helped him out.

'As for the question of Ginette Meurant, her brother-in-law talks about her as if she's a joke. Apparently, he said to Millard, when he left:

'"If you need a woman, there's always my little sister-in-law, who's married a fool and is bored."

'He swears there's nothing else. He gave him Ginette's address, adding that she loved going to a dance hall in Rue des Gravilliers.

'If he's to be believed, Pierre Millard gave no further sign of life, and nor did Ginette.'

That wasn't necessarily true, but it was plausible.

'What do I do with him?'

'Take his statement and let him go. But don't lose sight of him, because he'll be needed at the trial.'

If there was a trial. A new investigation would begin, as soon as Lapointe and Janvier brought Ginette Meurant into Maigret's office.

Would he be able to establish her complicity with her lover beyond any shadow of a doubt?

Nicolas Cajou would go and identify Millard's body, and then the chambermaid, and others.

Then would come the examination of the case, and then, possibly, the referral to the public prosecutor.

Meanwhile, it was more than likely that Ginette would remain in prison.

And then, one day, it would be her turn to appear before the court.

Maigret would be called as a witness once more. The jury would try to make sense of this story, which took place in a world so different from their own.

Before that, because the case was more straightforward and the timetable less busy at the Seine-et-Marne court, Maigret would be summoned to Melun.

He'd be shut up with other witnesses in a dark, muffled room like a sacristy where he would wait his turn watching the door and listening to the muted echoes from the courtroom.

He would see Gaston Meurant between two gendarmes, would swear to tell the truth, the whole truth and nothing but the truth.

Would he really divulge all? At a particular point, when the telephone was ringing non-stop in his office, from where he was in a way pulling the strings of all the characters, had he not taken upon himself a responsibility that was hard to explain?

Could he not have . . .

In two years' time, he would no longer have to worry

about other people's problems. He'd be living with Madame Maigret in an old house that resembled a presbytery, far from the Quai des Orfèvres and the law courts where men are judged. He'd spend hours on end sitting in a boat moored to a post, watching the water flow past and fishing.

His office was full of pipe smoke. Typewriters could be heard clacking in the adjoining office, telephones were ringing.

He was startled by a gentle tap on the door, which opened to reveal Lapointe's youthful physique.

Did he really recoil slightly, as if he were being asked to account for himself?

'She's here, chief. Do you want to see her straight away?'

And Lapointe waited, seeing that Maigret was slowly emerging from a dream – or a nightmare.

Night at the Crossroads

GEORGES SIMENON

She stepped forwards, her silhouette slightly blurred in the dim light. She stepped forwards like a film star, or rather, like the perfect woman of an adolescent's dream.

And her brother stood by her as a slave stands near the sovereign he is sworn to protect.

On the outskirts of Paris, a sensational crime in an isolated neighbourhood becomes the focus of Maigret's investigation. But the strange behaviour of an enigmatic Danish aristocrat and his reclusive sister prove to be even more troubling.

Translated by Linda Coverdale

OTHER TITLES IN THE SERIES

THE SAINT-FIACRE AFFAIR
GEORGES SIMENON

'Maigret savoured the sensations of his youth again: the cold stinging eyes, frozen fingertips, an aftertaste of coffee. Then, stepping inside the church, a blast of heat, soft light; the smell of candles and incense.'

The last time Maigret went home to the village of his birth was for his father's funeral. Now an anonymous note predicting a crime during All Souls' Day mass draws him back there, where troubling memories resurface and hidden vices are revealed.

Translated by Shaun Whiteside

OTHER TITLES IN THE SERIES

SIGNED, PICPUS
GEORGES SIMENON

'"It's a matter of life and death!" he said.

A small, thin man, rather dull to look at, neither young nor old, exuding the stale smell of a bachelor who does not look after himself. He pulls his fingers and cracks his knuckles while telling his tale, the way a schoolboy recites his lesson.'

A mysterious note predicting the murder of a fortune-teller; a confused old man locked in a Paris apartment; a financier who goes fishing; a South American heiress... Maigret must make his way through a frustrating maze of clues, suspects and motives to find out what connects them.

Translated by David Coward

OTHER TITLES IN THE SERIES

INSPECTOR CADAVER
GEORGES SIMENON

'To everyone, even the old ladies hiding behind their quivering curtains, even the kids just now who had turned to stare after they had passed him, he was the intruder, the undesirable.'

Asked to help a friend in trouble, Maigret arrives in a small provincial town where curtains twitch and gossip is rife. He also finds himself facing an unexpected adversary: the pale, shifty ex-policeman they call 'Inspector Cadaver'.

Translated by William Hobson

OTHER TITLES IN THE SERIES

MAIGRET SETS A TRAP
GEORGES SIMENON

'It was 4 August. The windows were wide open but brought no relief, since they allowed in even more warm air, which seemed to be rising from the melting tarmac, the burning hot stonework, and even the Seine itself: one could imagine the river steaming like a pan of water on a stove.'

Paris comes under siege when someone starts killing women on the streets one summer – and Maigret must hatch a plan to lure the murderer out.

Translated by Siân Reynolds

OTHER TITLES IN THE SERIES

MAIGRET ENJOYS HIMSELF
GEORGES SIMENON

'Here at his window in the middle of the morning, vaguely observing the comings and goings in the street, he had a feeling that reminded him of certain days in his childhood, when his mother was still alive and he was off school because he had the flu or it was the end of term. It was the feeling of finding out 'what went on when he wasn't there'.

Inspector Maigret is meant to be taking a holiday, but he can't resist following the development of his colleague Janvier's case in the papers – and playing a few tricks on the way.

Translated by David Watson

OTHER TITLES IN THE SERIES

MAIGRET'S DOUBTS
GEORGES SIMENON

'At this time the previous day he had never heard of the Martons, the train-set specialist was beginning to haunt his thoughts, and so was the elegant young woman who, he admitted, had boldly stood up to him when he had done everything he could to unsettle her.'

When a salesman from a Paris department store confides his secret fears to Maigret, the Inspector soon becomes caught up in a treacherous feud between husband and wife that is not as clear cut as it seems.

Translated by Shaun Whiteside

OTHER TITLES IN THE SERIES